Spaghetti Legs

Spaghetti Legs

JOHN LARKIN

A Mark Macleod Book
RANDOM HOUSE
AUSTRALIA

To my wife Jacqui. For all her love, encouragement, support, and cups of tea during the writing of this novel.

Thanks to Mark Macleod for his priceless editorial assistance.

A Mark Macleod Book
Random House Australia
an imprint of
Random House Australia Pty Ltd
20 Alfred Street, Milsons Point, NSW 2061

Sydney   New York   Toronto
London   Auckland
and agencies throughout the world

First published in 1993

National Library of Australia
Cataloguing-in-Publication Data

Larkin, John, 1963–
    Spaghetti legs.
    ISBN 0 09 182747 7.
    I. Title.
A823.3

Cover design by Mark Hand
Cover illustration by Craig Smith
Typeset by Midland Typesetters, Maryborough, Victoria
Printed by Australian Print Group, Victoria
Production by Vantage Graphics, Sydney.

Chapter 1

Toongabbie is the sort of suburb that you would ignore, unless your house happened to be in it. Just as you would overlook the house at number 15 York Crescent, unless you happened to live in it. And you would have gone out of your way to disregard the leg that held up the sheet and doona in the third bedroom of number 15 York Crescent, unless you happened to be attached to it.

Eric Underwood was attached to his leg, as he was to the other bits of his body. But his left leg held a special place in his heart. When he combined it with the other one it could propel him along fast. So far his left leg, helped along a bit by the right, had earned him a couple of gold medals for sprinting and an absolute bummer of a nickname.

It would have to be a strange set of circumstances that would force a serious athlete, such as Eric, to use one of the tools of his trade as a tent pole. But when Eric was upset he would retreat to his bed and let the world pass him by while he was tucked safe beneath the covers. His mother knew when he was coming out of the deep-blue-funk-zone when he started reading comics under the bedclothes with the aid of a torch and a leg.

The reason for Eric's gloom was the combined effect of spending his last day at primary school and losing his girlfriend.

He was looking forward to going to high school with a mixture of excitement and dread.

At primary school he was a fairly anonymous character who was only ever noticed at the school's athletic carnival once a year. For a week after the carnival he was a cult figure. The sort of guy that the other kids were proud to know. Some even pretended to know him just to impress their friends. He enjoyed it.

Because Eric was hopeless at football, couldn't swim for peanuts and hardly said boo to a mouse, he drifted back into obscurity for the rest of the year. But for one week, one mega-fantastic week each year, Eric was famous.

Now there would be no more Toongabbie Primary School athletic carnivals, just as there would be no more Toongabbie Primary. It was time to move on. And while Eric was prepared to take on what he thought would be the stronger and faster guys of high school, he was not prepared to do it without Sunflower Fox by his side.

Sunflower Fox was the most beautiful girl in 6-Red. No, let's go out on a limb here: the whole of year six.

When Eric first saw her, way back in second grade, he thought he had died and gone to heaven, it was so easy for him to imagine her sitting on a cloud, plucking a heavenly melody out of a harp.

Eric's parents had moved the family from Georges Hall during the summer holidays of that year. But the heartbreak he felt at having to leave his old school and friends behind was soon forgotten as he fell headlong into the emotional whirlpool of love.

Their eyes had first met over a Vegemite sandwich and her beauty was so amazing that Eric felt as if his heart was going to melt. There was something so haunting about her smile that it was easy to see how people got religion. Every time he looked at her he felt himself at one with the universe.

She was absolutely fautless. There was even something charming in the way she allowed chocolate Moove to dribble down her chin at recess, and she wore her sari with such poise and dignity that Eric half expected the principal to declare it standard school uniform.

Despite the fact that Eric felt his life could not go on until she was by his side, he kept his feelings well and truly hidden for fear of rejection.

Every day he walked dejectedly home from school and picked a flower while reciting the age-old mantra 'she loves me, she loves me not'. And he would grind any flower that informed him 'she loves me not' into a green, mushy pulp, his feelings were so intense. This practice went on for about two years until he got in trouble from Neighbourhood Watch for destroying the flower-beds in his street. Every night after that he poured out his feelings to his cat. They were just too intense to trust to another human.

At the start of year six when the teacher, Mr Finn, was deciding the girl–boy seating arrangements, Eric prayed to any god prepared to listen that his seat would be next to Sunflower Fox.

Eric's stomach did cartwheels and his mind a forward three and a half somersault when Mr Finn decided that it would.

However, having Sunflower next to him made it worse. It made him feel sick to be so near and yet so far.

The intensity grew to the point where, whenever he took his place next to her, he felt he was going to throw up. Hardly the feelings normally associated with love. If he had bought her a card at that point and poured out his true feelings, the card would have read something like: 'Dear Sunflower, every time I see you I feel like sticking my head down the toilet, love Eric'. Not exactly words to make her want to leap into his arms, but that's how he felt. He wasn't sure exactly where these emotions came from, but the mere sight of her made him want to puke.

Eventually, for the sake of his health, he realised that he had to find a way of talking to her without looking at her. After experimenting briefly with a paper bag and a couple of air holes, he came to the conclusion that it would be easier for all concerned if he just used the phone. So one night, after calling the three or four other Fox households in the Toongabbie area, he eventually got the right one and her liquid crystal voice was on the other end of the line.

'Hello?' said Sunflower.

Eric's hands were sweating so much that he had to hang up the phone before he dropped it. He went into the bathroom, wiped his hands and sprayed them with the type of drying powder normally associated with cuts. A short while later he'd built up enough courage to call her again.

'Hello?'

Eric felt the vibration of her voice all the way down to his feet and back up to his nose.

'Hello?' said Sunflower again.

'H . . .' said Eric so feebly that he sounded like a mouse with a sore throat.

'Hello? Beep. Beep. Beep. Beep.'

Eric thought that this was a curious thing for her to say until he realised that she must have hung up. With trembling hands he put down the receiver too.

To try and clear his thoughts, he took out the garbage, which he later got in trouble for, seeing it wasn't collection night. An hour later he had rallied and decided to give it one more try, only this time it must have been her father who answered.

Eric had no idea what a relic from the sixties was, but he was soon to find out.

'Yes like hello?'

Eric was too shy to speak, too stunned to hang up.

'Look man is there anybody there, like? Are you the dude who keeps hassling Sunflower on the phone? Like man what's up? And, while we're on the subject of movement, what goes down?'

Eric didn't understand most of what Mr Fox said, but nobody had ever called him a man before, and despite the fact that he couldn't get his mouth into working order, he felt rather grown up. But not quite grown up enough to speak.

'What gives, man? You ring up people and then listen to them, is that how you get your thrills? Or are you a deaf guy who keeps ringing the wrong number or something? I mean if they had an abusive phonecallers club they probably wouldn't let you join.'

Mr Fox burst out laughing, and Eric had to admit that the picture his mind was starting to paint of his future father-in-law was not a very good one. At least the mystery of why Sunflower wore a sari to school was explained.

'Yeah. Yeah that's right, dude, if they had an

abusive phonecallers club, they probably wouldn't let you join.'

Unfortunately Mr Fox's amusing line didn't get a follow up, so he merely repeated himself.

'Don't bother us again, dude, or I'll call the fuzz.'

At the thought of being a threat to the Fox family, Eric's lack of self-esteem collapsed further inwards and he slammed down the phone, knowing in his heart that Sunflower would never be his girlfriend.

The next day in class Eric sat at his desk totally dejected. Just when he was thinking of picking up his backpack and hurling it around the classroom to see the outcome, Sunflower passed him a note. It read: 'Did you call me last night Eric?'

His face turned a serious shade of green, but before he had a chance to vomit his Coco Pops all over the desk he grabbed his pen and wrote a large 'YES' under Sunflower's message.

Sunflower's reply was just as quick: 'I think you're cute, and I want you to be my boyfriend'.

The sun seemed to radiate new warmth. The trees whispered. The birds' chatter seemed, well it seemed something or other.

They became the talk of the school. The princess and the punk they were called, which did not upset

Eric as he liked his older sister's Sex Pistols records.

That had been only two months ago, and it seemed like eternity. This afternoon, as they walked out hand in hand from Toongabbie Primary for the last time, Eric gave Sunflower a kiss on the cheek and said, 'See you in six weeks, babe.'

Sunflower said that she would not be going to Pendle Hill High but to Catherine McCauley Girls' School and it cut Eric in half. She said that they would still see each other around, but they both knew that their lives would drift apart.

Eric spent the rest of the afternoon, after leaving school, heartbroken in bed, and only began to rally when the 'Bugs Bunny Show' started. He felt a strange affinity with Pepe Le Pew as he chased a cat, with a stripe of white paint down its back, around a heart-shaped island.

After the cartoons were finished, Eric sat up in bed, and came to the conclusion that he was too young to be reminiscing. So to console his broken heart, he slipped into the kitchen and ate a packet of Tim Tams.

After his stomach settled down he decided that he would allow himself to spend the whole weekend in bed, or at least playing computer games. On Monday, the start of the summer holidays, he would go and hang out with his best friend Ian Champion, and get some philosophical insight from Iggy Suede. And with that resolved he turned on the Derryn Hinch show just so he could be in the company of someone who was more annoyed than him.

Chapter 2

Snaking its way through the outskirts of Toongabbie, near Eric's home, is the cleverly named Toongabbie Creek. Loosely translated from the Aboriginal 'creek of much toxic waste', this stream becomes a raging torrent as it hurls its way through the suburbs and into Parramatta River in times of heavy rain.

The creek had changed a lot in recent years. In the old days all you needed for a day out down there was a butterfly net and a friend. These days a Geiger counter would be useful. The radioactive grasshoppers in the area have been known to leap thirteen kilometres at a single bound, making the one time-honoured art of bug-catching virtually impossible.

When the second wave of immigrants arrived

in Toongabbie in the early seventies to settle into their brand new three-bedroom houses, the only accident they could possibly have imagined their families being involved in was if a cow from one of the nearby herds went on a homicidal rampage. But now in the nineties the only people likely to find any cattle in Toongabbie would be arch-eologists.

Life, as they say, moves pretty fast. It's just a shame that some of the chemicals washed into the creek did not flow out as quickly.

Eric's house was in one of the better areas of Toongabbie; that is the residents of this area zip-started a better class of lawnmower on Sunday mornings. Their houses, or so they thought, were tidier, their cars shinier, and their skins less tattooed than those of that rabble from across Fitzwilliam Road.

Ian Champion's house was a two-minute bike ride or a ten-minute slog away from Eric's, depending on their mood or the transport available at the time. Apart from being Eric Underwood's best friend, Ian Champion was a genius, a real paste-eating sciencehead, heavily into microscopes and equilateral triangles. The sort of kid who either ends up an astrophysicist or a bum. While most of the students at Toongabbie Primary were making things with play-doh, Ian was busy trying to work out its scientific properties.

The Ian Champions of this world are usually born with glasses on. They're hopeless at sport—usually too busy trying to apply Pythagoras's theorem to a soccer ball to be bothered kicking it in the goal—and when they accidentally hit you in the groin with a loaded school bag, they can tell you exactly what is wrong with you and more specifically what treatment to apply in order to alleviate the pain.

While sitting quietly at their desks, people like Ian will casually announce that they can find, at any given moment, the precise location of Orion's Belt in the afternoon sky using a magnet and a toy compass. When Ian did this the teacher would casually adjust his stance and then fling a piece of chalk at the little smart alec. Ian would deflect the chalk with his glasses and comment on its beautiful flight, which invariably included a particularly attractive parabolic curve.

The fact that Ian's type end up being accountants rather than research scientists is a sad comment on our society's way of thinking. A partner at a large accounting company earns a hell of a lot more than the guy who is trying to plug up the ozone layer.

'Yeah sure the ozone layer is important, but is it cost effective?' young stockbrokers would scream at each other in the pub near the Sydney Stock Exchange.

When someone teased Ian about the thickness of his glasses, calling him 'Jam-jar Eyes', he would say, 'Yes, well, my glasses might be thick, but they let me see objects that would be otherwise out of focus.'

Ian didn't have many friends, but Eric was proud to say that he was one of them. He was not particularly smart, not like Ian was anyway, but they did have one thing in common that made them friends—the creek.

During the school holidays they would set off with their fishing lines, nets and a packed lunch and spend all day down there. Eric would be busy looking for insects and spiders while Ian kept looking for arthropods. Eric didn't think for one minute that they were looking for the same thing, although they had quite different intentions in mind. Eric wanted his spiders and insects to beat each other up, while Ian was busy trying to create a new super insect by cross breeding.

On the first Monday of the summer holidays, Eric got out of bed, washed his face, ate an industrial size bowl of Coco Pops and headed off with Ian, who had called right on nine o'clock.

Unlike Sunflower Fox, Ian had mentioned that he wouldn't be going to Pendle Hill High but to some science brain school. Neither of them knew the name. They knew, though, that this could be the last summer they would spend down the creek together and they wanted to make the most of it.

They spent the morning catching tadpoles, wrigglers, and at one point managed to corner a frill-necked lizard, which is quite a neat trick seeing creeks are notoriously short of corners. But in the end it darted away between some rocks and into its hole.

They were sitting on the bank cursing all things lizardy, and leafing through a nudey mag that they'd found stashed down there, when Eric noticed a wolf's hole under a huge gum tree. Ian said that there weren't any wolves in Toongabbie, so Eric said maybe it's here on holidays. They both fell about laughing hysterically.

Brushing off the dirt that was caused by rolling around on the ground in fits of laughter, they hid the mag in a better spot, wandered over to the gum tree and poked their heads down into the hole. Because it was too dark they couldn't see how far down it went. Ian said that it would be perfectly safe to go down into the hole as, judging by its dimensions, the only living thing that could have created it would have been a three-foot-wide tick, and as one of that width had not been found, even in America, they would be perfectly safe.

Eric and Ian raced home and each of them fished his father's torch out of the shed. Eric's father was a clerk and Ian's a research scientist, but they both had the old Eveready Dolphin torch.

Ten minutes later they turned on their torches and clambered down into the tunnel, Eric behind Ian. After scrambling on their hands and knees for about twenty metres they found themselves in a huge cathedral-like cave. After Eric's eyes adjusted he couldn't help but notice that the walls were writhing in a way that he was not sure he liked. He was about to say something stupid about moving walls when Ian calmly said, 'Bats.'

'Vampires!' screamed Eric. 'Let's get out of here!'

Ian blocked the exit and informed Eric that they were not vampire bats but fruit bats, and even if they were, vampire bats only attack cattle.

They moved on through the cave. Eric kept one eye on Ian, who led the way, and another nervous eye on the bats. Eric never had any reason to doubt him. Ian was always right. But just in case, he made a conscious effort not to make any mooooing noises as they moved about.

Despite the bats, Eric felt rather safe in the cave, sealed off from the outside world. No one could bully him, no one could pick on him, and no one could call him 'spaghetti legs' or 'stinky'.

Eric was tall, thin and seemed to have legs that stretched up to his chest, but despite that, he felt the only reason some of the other kids at school called him 'spaghetti legs' was because they were jealous of his athletic ability. 'Stinky', though, was a home-grown nickname and came from his reluctance to take showers. His older sister, Jenny, had once convinced him that a man lived down the drain and one day when she was having a shower he had put his hand up and tried to pull her down. Fortunately she managed to fight him off with her toothbrush and curling wand. For some reason this scare left her emotionally scarred and strangely short of cash. So to ease her torment she made Eric give her his pocket money each week. In return she wouldn't tell their mother that when Eric went into the bathroom all he did was turn on the shower and make fake cleaning noises. Using this technique Eric could often go two weeks at a time without washing. After this his socks would begin to defy gravity and the dog would start following him around. When this happened his mother would order him into the bath and threaten to scrub a layer of skin off him if he didn't come out sparkling clean.

All this was long before he'd won Sunflower Fox's heart. When that happened he didn't care what horrors the shower held, he was determined to smell nice for his girlfriend, but even years later the nickname was hard to shake.

'Let's go home,' said Ian, breaking into Eric's thoughts. 'It's getting late, we'll come back tomorrow and spend the whole day exploring.'

They emerged from the tunnel, and covered the entrance with branches and leaves. Ian was certain the bats used another entrance, and as they'd never heard stories of bats dive-bombing a gum tree, he was probably right again.

After dinner, Eric went to bed and played tunnelling games under his doona, in the wardrobe, and under the bed. He imagined that the bowels of the cave contained unbelievable wealth, fantastic treasure, and some interesting fossils for Ian and his dad. Deep, deep into the cave there would be an underground river with sailing boats that would take them to far-off lands where men in baggy satin trousers with huge swords would look at them in dangerous ways.

The following day it rained, so Eric stayed in his bedroom. He kept himself amused playing computer games with the cat.

It rained solidly for a week. Eric heard that someone tried to cross the flooded bridge in their car and had been swept away. Toongabbie was on the evening news. This only seemed to happen when somebody died. Eric was just glad that the camera crew did not reveal the whereabouts of their cave.

The rain eventually eased and the creek returned to its passive self.

The next day Eric waited for Ian at the entrance to the cave with his torch, a packed lunch, and some garlic—he still wasn't entirely convinced that they weren't vampire bats. But Ian didn't come.

In the evening Eric rode his bike round to Ian's house but found it deserted. There was a vandalised 'FOR SALE' sign in the garden.

Chapter 3

Three weeks into the summer holidays and despite what the forecasters said, the rain, which had returned the day after Ian Champion's family left, showed no signs of abating. The climatic conditions only made Eric's gloom worse—he was sure that the low pressure front was centred directly over his bed.

The holidays were not going well at all. He had lost his girlfriend, his best friend, and to make matters worse his sister was going out with a complete moron named Stevo the Rev.

Eric's father was also in a dangerous mood. Apart from the fact that he couldn't get out and enjoy his one passion of gardening, Stevo the Rev had left the Monaro ticking over for far too long the previous night. Mr Underwood had bitten his lip for a while but after listening to a purring V-8 get drowned out by Guns 'N' Roses for an hour, he burst out and told Stevo just where he was going to stick his twin exhausts if he didn't turn the bloody engine off immediately.

This had greatly upset Jenny Underwood. She had gone crying to her mother, who agreed that, with the exception of Stevo the Rev, all men were bastards.

The mood in the Underwood household the following morning could not be described as pleasant. The women weren't talking to the men, nobody appeared to be talking to Eric, even Eric's five-year-old brother Paul was throwing his Lego around with a little more anger than usual.

After breakfast Eric retreated to the relative sanctuary of his room and spent the morning watching music videos. He only got up twice: once for M.C. Hammer, and a little later on for Black Box. He honestly believed that if Sunflower Fox could see him dance she would leap back into his arms.

Three boring songs later Eric drifted back into the zzzzzzz zone and was having a great dream that he and Sunflower were married and they were on their way to visit Ian in his lab where he had just invented a gigantic plug for the ozone layer, when Jenny stormed into his bedroom. She was wearing a look of 'don't mess with me, matey' on her face.

Jenny's teenage wardrobe had long ago burst at the seams and she had simply moved all of the clothes that weren't in the first team into Eric and Paul's. The wardrobe was just about off limits for hide 'n' seek nowadays, as it was stuffed full of Jenny's things.

'What do you want?' said Eric, smacking his lips together.

'My jeans if it's any of your business, snothead. Anyway, what are you sooking about?'

'I'm not sooking, it's raining so I can't go out.'

'That's not it at all. Mum said you were sooking because you broke up with your girlfriend and your weirdo mate Ian moved.'

'Get out, grease-monkey!'

Eric knew that he was taking a risk by calling his sister a grease-monkey, but she had hit the first low blow and although she was seventeen and much stronger than him, well, if she wanted a piece of the action he reckoned that he could give her and her revhead of a boyfriend heaps.

'*Mum!*' yelled Jenny. '*Eric's just called me a grease-monkey.*'

Eric could hear his mother's slippers clomping dangerously through the house.

'What's going on in here, you pair?'

'He called me a grease-monkey, Mum.'

'Yeah, but she said that I broke up with Sunflower and Ian had moved.'

'Well you have and he did.'

'But she said I was sooking because of it.'

'You are. And there's nothing wrong with a girl being a mechanic, you were the one who bought Jenny and Stevo matching oil rags for Christmas, remember? Now apologise to your sister!'

'But she . . .'

'I don't care what she. You apologise!'

'Oh all right. I'm sorry, Thing.'

'ERIC!'

'I'm sorry, Jenny.'

'With sugar on top.'

'That's enough, Jenny! Get whatever it is you're getting and leave Eric alone.' Mrs Underwood should have been working for the United Nations.

An angry silence hung in the air as Jenny kept looking for her jeans. Eventually they turned up.

'No wonder you couldn't find them,' said Eric, 'there's more hole than jean, who are you going out with? Freddy Krueger?'

'Be original, loser! Been listening to Dad again?'

'Where's Stevo taking you anyway? A tyre screeching exhibition?'

'Hey Eric?'

'What?'

'You stink.' And with this parting shot she slammed the door shut and went back to her room to change.

'*I don't stink any more*,' yelled Eric across three rooms.

'I think we had our three kids too far apart,' Mrs Underwood said to her husband as they read the papers.

'I think we had three kids too many,' he said. They both burst out laughing and offered to make each other a cup of coffee.

Eric sat quietly fuming in bed. Why couldn't people just leave him alone? As far as he was concerned, everyone was entitled to a bit of sulking every now and again. Even Gandhi must have had the odd sulk or two.

Eric looked at the poster of Gandhi on his wall. It wasn't really Gandhi, but some English actor dressed up to look like him. He'd put it there after he and Iggy Suede had watched the film a couple of years ago. They both thought he was great.

Ten minutes later, Eric was walking down the road in the pouring rain. He decided that he'd had enough family life for one day, and what he needed was a bit of Iggy Suede's philosophy to cheer him up.

Iggy Suede was a seventeen-year-old contradiction. He was a complete set of conflicting emotions, attitudes, looks, and pimples stuffed into a flannelette shirt. He was heavily into Iron Maiden and Vivaldi which explained, in part, the black T-shirt and violin earring. When he didn't have his head buried in a heavy metal magazine, it was between the pages of the collected works of great European writers. This confused his teachers. They were used to their male students making verbal references to footballers. It came as a bit of a shock when they heard someone quoting Chekhov and Kafka at them. They didn't have a clue what he was talking about, and to cover their embarrassment they usually suggested that he shut up.

Iggy hated stereotypes. He felt that being brainy was not enough reason to go out and buy a backpack and start covering his books with plastic. He thought his duffle bag was good enough for carting his belongings around in and that heavy metal posters made ideal book covers. Iggy had been in Jenny Underwood's year at high school, but she left to do a tech course in motor mechanics. That's where she met Stevo the Rev. Iggy, on the other hand, was determined to get into university and to study English literature. The rejection heaped upon Iggy by his teachers and fellow students left him with plenty of time to study, and he topped year eleven in both English and History.

Just when people thought they had Iggy's personality worked out, he would do something unexpected like go to a rugby league match and cheer the ref.

Like Eric, Iggy was a loner. But whereas Iggy was a loner by his own choosing, which gave him more time to read and listen to his Madonna and Metallica CDs, Eric would have liked to be part of the crowd. It's just that he didn't have a crowd to be part of. His circle of friends appeared to be shrinking daily. Pretty soon he would have to stop calling it his circle of friends and start referring to it as a triangle.

Eric liked Iggy because he was so together he didn't care what people thought about him. Iggy liked his young neighbour because 'the little dude was so intense'.

Iggy's mother answered when Eric knocked. She was a small woman of forty who, like Sunflower Fox's parents, looked like she lived in a time warp. Any minute she might have been about to reach for a tambourine and burst into a chorus of some old Beatles' song like 'All you need is love'. Her skin was so white she had obviously spent a lot of time looking for fossils in Arctic caves. She looked permanently confused, which could have been caused by living alone with Iggy. He seemed to confuse everybody except Eric.

'Iggy's not in, Eric. He's gone to see Madonna.'

Eric didn't know that Madonna was in town. If he did he would like to have gone too.

'Where is she playing, Mrs Suede?' asked Eric, who could not bring himself to call her Rainbow-Fish despite being told to several times.

'Over umm, let me think. Iggy did tell me. Umm, it's over there,' she said, pointing towards the linen closet.

Eric felt that it was unlikely that Madonna or anybody else for that matter would hold a concert anywhere in Toongabbie. And despite the natural acoustics that the venue obviously offered, he doubted very much that Madonna would be doing a gig in the Suedes' linen closet.

'Where?'

'Oh yeah, I remember: Paris.'

'Paris? Iggy's gone to Paris?'

'Yeah, he's gone to see Chekhov's grave as well.'

'But Iggy said that's in Russia.'

Eric walked back home very unhappy. He sloshed up the hallway to his bedroom.

'*Eric, your shoes are soaking wet!!!*' yelled his mother.

A couple of kilometres away, a cow that was standing alone in a field looked round, confused, and wondered where all the noise was coming from.

After Eric had put his shoes outside and mopped the polished wooden floor, he slid back up the hall in his socks. Unfortunately he underestimated his speed, whizzed past his bedroom and crashed into the telephone table. The impact brought down his mother's favourite painting, which was hung by the laundry door.

'Eric Underwood, I've just about had enough of you for one day. Why don't you go into your room and read Iggy's letter?'

Eric quickly untangled himself from the telephone cord and slid excited into his room. He didn't stop to think that there weren't any mail deliveries on Saturdays and that Jenny had obviously been hiding his letter for the past couple of days. Iggy had sent him a letter. That was the only thing worth considering.

Dear Eric,

How's it going little bro'? You're not going to believe this, dude, but I'm in Paris. I came to say goodbye but you were down the creek with Ian and I couldn't find you.

Paris is great, it's full of people who look like they're about to finish their coffee and go off and write a Pulitzer prize winner. I've never seen so many cafes in my life, caffeine addiction must be a real problem in this city.

I can't believe the size of my hotel room. I have to drop breadcrumbs behind me to find my way back to it each day. I feel a little bit guilty about being an expert on the rise of the proletariat while at the same time staying in such opulence, but I'll get over it.

I'm going to Moscow the day after tomorrow to visit some famous graves but I'll be back a couple of days before school starts.

Gotta go, I'm a bit short of cash so I'm going to go and withdraw some money from the Left

Bank (ha ha ha).

See you in two weeks.

Regards,
Iggy

Iggy's letter sent Eric's mind racing.

Not being a big fan of actually doing things, Eric would often just send his mind off on adventures while he was tucked safely under his doona with a comic and a packet of Tim Tams. The adventures always included journeys through backless wardrobes, bottomless wishing wells, and turtleless drains. His free floating imagination would always arrive back from the ends of the universe with a million stories to tell and claiming to have met Mr Spock.

With Sunflower and Ian gone, and Iggy traipsing around European cemeteries, Eric realised any entertainment before school went back was up to him.

He also realised it was time to start making some career choices. Iggy was obviously going to be a novelist and Ian was sure to invent something incredibly useful, but what about him? His mother and father never really took much interest in his school work. As long as he didn't burn down the classroom and arrived home alive each day, as far as they were concerned he was doing okay.

At the start of year 6, Mr Underwood asked Eric what he wanted to be when he grew up. Being a big fan of Batman, Eric said that he wanted to be just like the caped crusader, or failing that he would like to become a spy.

Due to the fact that an exciting advertisement appeared on tv in the middle of their conversation, Mr Underwood never got to voice any disapproval of this career choice.

Although the cold war was well and truly over, Moscow still conjured up images of cloaks, daggers and secret documents.

Eric put Iggy's letter in his bottom drawer. And after watching the exploits of Boris and Natasha on the Rocky and Bullwinkle show, decided that he would definitely become a spy.

Being a realist he was well aware that he would need to get some practical experience before he could apply to the government for a job.

A few days later, after reading his sister's diary and sabotaging his brother's massive Lego construction so that the roof imploded when touched, Eric had pretty well exhausted the possibilities for spying in his house and had to look further afield.

He discovered to his immense surprise that Basil the dog had bones buried in the backyard. This would not have caused too much interest in most households, but when you looked at them from the air (on top of the carport roof) the burial markings formed what appeared to be part of a pattern. Basil was accused of sending messages to enemy satellites, put under heavy surveillance and had his Meaty Bite intake closely monitored.

This was all good fun and kept Eric and Basil amused. But it wasn't until the new neighbour moved in that things started to get serious spywise.

Chapter 4

Neighbours are weird. You are forced to be friendly with them for no other reason than the sharing of a common boundary. There are of course exceptions to this rule: North and South Korea for one springs readily to mind. Throughout history, neighbours have shared tea, sugar, dog stories, and a mutual hatred for the people across the road with the loud music. This friendship goes on for years until they move out and another lot arrive with a whole new set of sugar borrowing stories.

Eric's was a normal neighbourhood. Every house had 2.5 kids, 1.5 dogs, 1.2 cats and the lounge room built around the tv.

When the Keegans moved out, the Underwoods all took turns waiting by the window for the removalist's van to arrive and pour out their new neighbours. It never came. Instead there was a procession of multi-coloured station wagons coming and going at all hours.

Mr Underwood's worst fears looked as if they'd be realised when on the first night the new neighbours had a barbecue and sang far too many verses of 'Blowing in the Wind' for his liking.

'As if it's not bad enough having the Suedes down the road, now we've got hippies next door,' he said and charged out of the house to set up a security system for his vegetable patch.

He needn't have worried. After the marshmallow and tambourine house-warming party, the Underwoods soon realised that they only had one new neighbour—a mop of stringy hair and hippy clothes—called Liz.

Lizard, as Mr Underwood referred to her, looked like someone who was always in a hurry. This was either because she was a very busy person, or she had no concept of time. They found out it was her concept of time when on one of her first days in the neighbourhood she walked home from the shops with Mrs Underwood. Eric's mother had innocently asked if Liz knew what time it was. Liz's reply was that time was just more evidence of fascist mind control. Mrs Underwood agreed that this could well be the case, but she was in a hurry to get home for the afternoon soapies.

Liz looked completely out of place in three-bedroomed suburbia. The Underwoods could not work out why someone who would gladly have given up her tie-dyed T-shirt collection to live in an alley in Paris could possibly choose to live in the suburbs.

For all her frizzy hair and seriously weird dress sense she was very attractive and Eric soon developed a massive crush on her.

Since he'd broken up with Sunflower, Eric had sworn off girls for the rest of his life. But that had been a couple of weeks ago and he hadn't reckoned on a total babe in dreadlocks moving in next door. And whereas Sunflower was a gorgeous looking girl of twelve, Liz was a gorgeous looking older woman with all her proper bits sticking out. She must have been at least nineteen. He didn't know if it was love. But he felt sick to his stomach every time he saw her.

Although his parents had nothing much to do with their new neighbour, Eric was determined to find out all he could about her.

Liz left for work, or for wherever it was she went each day, at around nine o'clock. Eric watched her dart out of the house at ten past nine, waited a few minutes then jumped over the side fence and let himself in through her rear window. He noticed a painting hung out to dry on the line.

She had a telescope positioned at the window and when Eric looked through it he found that it pointed at the surrounding houses rather than the sky.

Her house had hardly any furniture. A couple of chairs, a few flea-bitten bean bags and an old stereo made up the lounge room. The main bedroom contained the telescope and a bed. Her clothes were all over the place. The second bedroom consisted of just an old rug and heaps of incense sticks. The third bedroom had an easel in it, some painting equipment and a huge stack of books.

After about an hour of poking around Eric felt that he'd had enough adventure for one day and let himself out through the window. He carefully sealed up the flyscreen as he had done a hundred times before on his own bedroom window. He couldn't help having a look at the painting on the line. It depicted rows and rows of houses that all looked the same, going as far as to have a clothes-line full of nappies in each backyard. It didn't inspire him much, so he went home.

When Eric walked into his house he found that Paul was crying because the roof of his Lego mansion had collapsed on the beetles he had inside, and Jenny was furious because somebody had read her diary.

Eric slunk guiltily into his bedroom. And as the storm clouds gathered in the west, he put on his walkman in an attempt to shut out the thunder from the sky and the commotion from the lounge room.

The next day, Eric left the house and returned to his spy-making. He let himself in and was content to just relax on Liz's bed and look through her books.

As he was leaving at lunchtime he noticed that there were two more paintings hung out to dry. A quick glance revealed that they were only of people's backyards again. He was about to walk away when he noticed that one of the paintings detailed Mr Bell, from down the road, hurriedly leaving by the Fogarty's back door as Mr Fogarty was pulling his car into the driveway. He looked back at the first painting and saw what looked like Mrs Graham paying the milkman, but he realised that it was the milkman who was handing over money to Mrs Graham.

This went on for the next two weeks. Each day Eric let himself into Liz's house, looked through the telescope at the detailed lives of their neighbours and learnt something new about his neighbourhood on the way out. The Hill's Hoist had never revealed so much.

Two days before Iggy was supposed to return, Eric had just made himself comfortable on Liz's bed when he heard a key in the front door. He didn't have time to get out, so he dropped the book he was reading and hid under the bed.

Eric could hear Liz pottering around first in the bathroom and then the kitchen before she came into the bedroom a short while later. The bedspread didn't touch the floor and through the small gap he could see her feet walking all over the place until finally she leapt onto the bed.

The springs sagged so badly that they pushed into his face. He was able to turn his head sideways in order to breathe, but apart from that made no other movement.

Finally Liz's breathing changed as she fell into a deep sleep.

Eric crawled out from under the bed like a guilty crab and quietly fled. This time he ignored the information packed paintings that dangled from the clothesline.

The next day he let himself in by the normal method. He was shaken, but he refused to let one small scare interrupt a promising career in international espionage.

After a few hours he let himself out again and thought that with Iggy due to return any minute and the end of the school holidays it would be his last visit for a while.

The painting on the line was hung up sideways so he had to cock his head on one side to look at it. It was a painting of Liz lying on her bed. There was something beneath the bed that he couldn't quite work out. A face maybe. To his immense horror, Eric realised it was himself.

Liz came over unexpectedly in the evening to see Mr and Mrs Underwood. Surprisingly she hadn't come over to complain about Eric ransacking her house, but to invite the family to an exhibition that she was holding in an inner-city art gallery. She told them about her plans to live and work in Paris when the exhibition was over. And with the polite exchange of addresses, that they all knew they would never use, the neighbours said goodbye at the Underwoods' front door.

'Oh by the way, Liz, what's your exhibition called?' asked Mrs Underwood.

'The Hidden Suburbs,' said Liz. And she walked across the front lawn and out of their lives.

Chapter 5

The scare of being found out by Liz in such a demeaning way made Eric decide to give up being a spy and become something else instead. He felt that if he couldn't put one over on a paint-drunk hippy, he was unlikely to get the better of any trained enemy he was sure his spying skills would be pitted against.

When Liz had been in the lounge room talking to his parents, Eric spent the time moving from under his bed to the wardrobe and back again in search of the perfect hiding spot. Under the bed proved to be not such a good idea because in the darkness he rested his head against a pair of damp and slightly mouldy pyjama pants. He had hidden them under the bed after wetting them a couple of weeks earlier, dreaming about Sunflower Fox.

The wardrobe wasn't an appropriate hiding place either. After he'd disentangled himself from Jenny's massive collection of clothes he heard a distinctive growl. When his heart had stopped pounding he realised that it was just the deep contented purring of his cat, Kitty.

Eric didn't want to begin to imagine how much trouble he was going to be in now that he'd been sprung spying on Liz. Only a few weeks earlier, after he'd finished his chores, he had been grounded for a fortnight for using steel wool to scrub some stubborn mark off his parents' car. But this was break and enter. He was sure they would tie him to a bed until he was sixteen and beat him senseless on the hour.

In the end he couldn't stand the waiting any longer and had burst out into the lounge room and shouted, 'Okay I admit it, I'm guilty.' This caused a great deal of confusion for everyone.

'Okay Eric, I give up. What is it that you're guilty of?' said Mr Underwood between sips of coffee.

Totally fazed, Eric looked around the room. Not only was Liz not there, she appeared not to have mentioned his crime either.

In the end he admitted to sabotaging Paul's Lego and reading Jenny's diary.

His parents both had a laugh and told him not to do it again, which Eric thought showed a distinct lack of consistency in their punishment system.

Later on that evening, as the moon shone clear and bright over Toongabbie, Eric went to bed thinking that it was far out that Liz hadn't dobbed on him. He looked forward excitedly to Iggy's return the next day.

Chapter 6

Eric leapt out of bed at six in the morning and rang the airport. He spoke, or rather listened, to a recorded message about flight numbers and various arrival times. There had been no reference to Paris by the recorded voice and it became pretty clear that anybody who wanted flight information had to do a fair bit of homework before making the call.

Eric's Uncle Tim had once come out from England for a brief visit and he remembered that Tim's flight had arrived at around nine o'clock.

If he allowed Iggy's mother about an hour to drive the old Honda Civic back from the airport, Iggy would be pretty tired after a twenty-hour flight, so say give him half an hour to rest. Eric reckoned he could call on Iggy at about ten thirty and fill him in on all the goss of the area, particularly the brief stay of Liz.

Eric usually loved Sunday mornings. He would lie in bed until about seven, make mental threats to the paper boy and more particularly his whistle, go back to sleep, then finally get up at around ten to devour his bacon and eggs before hauling himself back to bed to watch the sports shows on tv.

But this Sunday morning had begun to drag.

After unsolving and re-solving his old Rubik's cube a couple of times, Eric whiled away a good chunk of the morning flicking lint balls into a set of imaginary goal posts on his bed. Finally, after psyching himself up for a couple of hours, he plucked up enough courage to smuggle both sets of pyjama pants out into the washing machine, because it had happened again that night.

Eventually, and to his everlasting relief, the Olde English clock in the lounge room struck ten thirty.

Eric casually put on his shoes, strolled out of the front door, and bolted down to the Suedes' house full of news and questions for Iggy.

'Oh hi, Eric,' said Mrs Suede at Eric's excited beatings on the front door. 'Come in.'

Eric walked straight into the Suedes' lounge

room. It was full of suitcases and packing crates. Iggy had sure taken a lot of stuff.

'Is Iggy in bed, Mrs Suede?'

'No?' She looked confused.

Eric could hardly tell the difference between Mrs Suede's confused look and her normal one, so he made no comment.

'Where is he then?'

'Iggy wrote to you didn't he?'

'Yeah, he sent me a letter from Paris.'

'But he sent you a second letter as well?'

'No.' Eric was beginning to get a sneaky suspicion that Jenny might have hidden it in revenge for him reading her diary.

'I think you had better sit down, Eric.'

Eric looked around the room for somewhere to park. There weren't many choices. He had read in his father's *Time* magazines that poachers were killing elephants in order to sell their ivory on the black market, so he made a small protest by not sitting on the upturned, plastic, elephant-foot umbrella holder. Instead he made himself as comfortable as possible on an old mahogany tea-chest.

'Iggy's not coming home, Eric.'

'What?'

'I'm sorry, love. He won't be back.'

'But all his stuff's here,' said Eric, nodding at Iggy's half unpacked books, posters and clothes.

'Yes Eric I know, it's both our stuff. I'm not unpacking, I'm packing. I'll be joining him.'

'You're going to live in Paris?'

'Not Paris, London.'

'But, but why?'

'Iggy wrote to me and said that he wouldn't be coming home. He also said he'd written a couple of letters to you. I thought it would have been hard for him to save for a trip like that, what with him only working part time in the library and the video store. He only bought himself a one-way ticket.'

'But who's he staying with?'

'My friends in London for the time being until I get over there and get us our own place.

'See Eric, I used to be a writer just like Iggy wants to be. I lived in London and I was quite successful. Of course my name wasn't Rainbow-Fish Suede then, it was something much more amusing.'

'Wha . . .?' It was hard to believe.

'Gwendamere Ramsbottom. Anyway, after I met my boyfriend, Ignatius Hollingsworth Junior, we decided to change our names. We then set off travelling around the world and got married. Unfortunately he was killed in a parachuting accident just after Iggy was born and I haven't written a word since. I think Iggy felt that if he went to Paris, Moscow and London it might inspire me and get me writing again. I don't know if it will but he's not coming back and I'm sick of disappointing him. So the only way of finding out is by going back to London.'

'But what about the house? Have you sold it?'

'It's not ours, it never was, we were renting. I only expected to stay for a couple of months until Iggy was born, but it ended up being eighteen years. I guess I've been hiding.

'All I know now, Eric, is that I've got to get my life in order or I'll lose the only thing that matters to me.'

'Iggy?'

'Iggy.'

'Your wardrobe needs an overhaul for a start,' said Eric, pointing at her crimplene flares and quoting directly from his father.

'A lot of me needs an overhaul,' said Mrs Suede laughing, 'I'm just glad I've got a second chance. You know Iggy could have stayed here, got into uni and done really well for himself. But he believes

in me enough to sacrifice all of it. I owe it
to start living again.'

After a hug and kiss Eric left the Suedes' house
for the last time. He'd spent so many happy times
in that little fibro box, and now some other family
would move in and stamp their personality on it.
He also realised that unless they had a young boy
in the family he would no longer be welcome in
it, despite playing a major part in its history.

As Eric dragged himself home he wondered why
all this was happening to him. He looked at the
clouds. He could not remember seeing the sun once
these summer holidays.

Eric tried to think about all the good times he'd
spent with Ian and Iggy. There was that time he
and Ian were hot on the trail of some Argentine
ants which they thought were valuable. They had
followed one from just near Ian's house to the creek
and felt they were getting pretty close to the nest.
Unfortunately just before they hit pay-dirt they
stumbled on the two toughest guys in school and,
more crucially, their cigarette stash.

Eric had wanted to bolt because he was much
faster than either Billy Nelson or Greg Fern, but
he was well aware that Ian wasn't.

Ian tried to stand up to their bullying, and as Eric

remembered later, had in fact thrown the first punch. But neither of them was cut out for fighting and they'd taken quite a beating. It finished with them both having their faces rubbed in some dog dirt.

Eric remembered they had half dragged their sorry selves home when Iggy had come skateboarding up to them, having just got back from Parramatta Library.

'What's happened to you two? It looks like you've been dragged backwards through dog shit.'

'We have.' Ian wiped the blood from his nose. 'There's a couple of thugs from school down the creek and we caught them smoking.'

'Who are they?'

'Billy Nelson and Greg Fern. Why?' asked Eric.

'Just testing the water. I know them, they've both got older brothers in high school, but I can handle them. C'mon, Nelson and Fern are dead meat.'

Iggy's revenge wasn't violent, nor was it even painful for the two thugs. It was better than that.

Nelson and Fern had seen what they were up against and they knew just how to play it. They were well aware of the laws of the jungle, having set most of them in Toongabbie Primary. They knew Iggy Suede was a dangerous animal and they did everything he commanded.

They kissed the soles of Ian and Eric's shoes, scooped mud into their half-full cigarette packets and waded through the creek wearing nothing but their underpants. And after Iggy had threatened to half kill them, assured him that that was the end of it and they wouldn't even look sideways at Eric and Ian in the playground.

'*Eric. Watch out for the garden gnome,*' said Mr Underwood and Eric was immediately jerked out of his stupor after walking home from the Suedes' house on autopilot. 'I'm moving them around to try and stop the cats bogging in the flower beds.'

'You want cats to think the gnomes are people?'

'Why not? It works for crows.'

Eric had always thought his father was a strange man. At least now he had concrete proof.

Chapter 7

'Okay, *where is it*?' yelled Eric at anyone who happened to be in the lounge room after he had finished slamming the front door.

'Don't come in here slamming doors and yelling at people, Eric!' said Mrs Underwood.

'Mrs Suede just told me that Iggy wrote me another letter.'

'No! He only sent you one letter. Old Rainbow-Fish must have been confused. She's good at that.'

'He wrote another letter as well to tell me that he wouldn't be coming home ever again.'

Suddenly Mrs Underwood understood Eric's anger.

'Somebody has read my letter and hidden it from me.'

Mrs Underwood, Eric, Jenny and Paul all had their own ideas just who that somebody was.

'Have you got Eric's letter, Jenny?' Mrs Underwood was taking the bull by the horns.

'So what if I have? It's only from that weirdo Iggy Suede.'

'You're the one who's weird, you grease sniffing bush pig! Iggy's really intelligent and stuff.'

'Yeah right, and I'll get you for what you just said, Spaghetti Legs. Anyway, Mum,' said Jenny, turning away from her seething brother, 'Eric read my diary.'

'This is different. Eric's friend has written what is obviously a very important letter. You on the other hand leave your diary around for everybody to read.'

'Read it have you, Mum?' said Jenny sarcastically.

'Don't be smart with me, girl! As big as you are I can still put you over my knee,' said Mrs Underwood, resorting to a bit of postwar child-rearing philosophy. 'Get to your room! And give Eric his letter!'

Neither Eric nor his mother trusted Jenny on this issue so they followed her as far as the hallway.

'Here's your stupid letter, loser.'

Eric snatched the letter from Jenny's hand, but she kept quite a tight hold, so all he was able to snatch was half of it.

The years of being picked on, abused and generally ignored by Jenny welled up inside him. His blood boiled, his nostrils flared, he carefully drew back his fist and clobbered her.

It was one of those punches that starts at your ankles, makes its way over your head and usually lands nowhere near its intended victim who, by this time, has usually walked away. But Eric wasn't so lucky. It whizzed past Jenny's chin, but the immense follow-through got his father right in the gut. He'd wandered in from the garden to see what all the racket was about and went down like a sack of potatoes.

'*I hate all of you*,' yelled Eric gathering up his shredded letter from the floor. He charged into his room and slammed the door behind him, breaking the loudest door-slam record previously held by Jenny.

'What was all that about?' asked Mr Underwood, not unreasonably. He'd arrived latest on the scene and come off worst.

'Let's go into the lounge room for a chat, shall we?' he said to the rest of the family. 'You too, Jenny!'

'No way, I'm going out with Stevo.' And with this Jenny charged into her room, picked up her bag and raced outside just as Stevo the Rev came screeching around the corner.

When Stevo's Monaro could no longer be seen or (more importantly) heard, Mr and Mrs Underwood went into the kitchen and made a cup of tea in an attempt to calm themselves down.

'I feel really sorry for Eric,' said Mrs Underwood.

'Why?'

'He broke up with his girlfriend, Ian's family have moved and left no forwarding address, and now he's just found out that Iggy's not coming home.'

'I never knew he even had a girlfriend.'

'Yeah. She's called Sunflower Fox.'

'The old son of a gun,' said Mr Underwood, giving his ego a pat on the head.

'He didn't talk about her much. Well, you know what Jenny's like.'

'I certainly do.'

'Anyway, she's going to a different high school, so that's that I'm afraid.'

'Well, he'll meet lots of new girls at Pendle Hill.'

'I know, but he's had his heart broken and on top of that he's lost his two best friends.'

'I think sometimes we forget the little guy. Well, I know I do.'

'Me too. I think we spoil Jenny because she's

the eldest and Paul because he's the baby. Poor old Eric often gets left to do his own thing.'

'What can we do?'

'Well for a start we can make him a big gooey chocolate cake.'

'That won't solve his problems.'

'No, but it might cheer him up a bit.'

So as Mr and Mrs Underwood busied themselves cracking eggs and whipping cream, Eric read Iggy's sticky-taped letter, secure in the knowledge that his outburst had ensured him, amongst other things, at least a bit of privacy.

In the letter Iggy told Eric all about his plans and how he didn't mean to deceive him. He was doing it for his mother, who had once been a promising young author but was now forty going on sixty. Iggy promised to keep in touch, gave Eric his address in London, and asked him to pass on his best wishes to his family and Ian.

Eric would have liked to pass on many things to Ian, including his own address, but the logistics of the whole business were beyond him at this stage. He'd looked in the white pages under the heading Champion, but according to Telecom they were still residents of Toongabbie. Maybe they'd be in the next directory.

At least he had Iggy's address so he'd be able to write often.

A couple of hours later Eric's parents came into his room. He looked up from the book he was reading and saw them standing over him with a huge chocolate cake. Paul was hovering in the background, obviously hoping for a piece.

'What's this for? It's not my birthday.'

'We know you've had a bit of a hard time of it lately, and we haven't always been there for you,' said his mother.

Eric wanted to cry. Instead he said, 'Thanks, I'll come out for some later.'

Chapter 8

As far as Eric was concerned the school holidays were over the day he found out that Iggy wasn't coming back. After that he'd spent the last week of the summer vacation listening to his walkman and playing computer games. He only left the house twice. The first was when he went for a ride around to his auntie's house for a scone attack, and the other was for a visit to the creek.

In a moment of total boredom he'd wandered down to the creek for old time's sake. But it had changed. It was no longer full of secret places and interesting insects. It was not just a storm-water outflow. Part of his past now, he wanted nothing more to do with it. He was about to turn around and wander back home when he saw a puff of smoke halfway down the bank. Eric wasn't sure whether

Billy Nelson and Greg Fern knew about Iggy's departure but he wasn't taking any chances and overtook the milk truck hurrying to get back home.

On the last Sunday morning before school started back, Eric was woken by his sister's sobbing. Still with his doona wrapped around him, he staggered out to the lounge room. 'What's the matter with Jenny, Dad?'

'She's broken up with Stevo. Didn't you hear all the racket last night?'

'No.'

Jenny and Stevo had called it quits around midnight the previous night. Jenny wanted more from the relationship than drag races and drive-ins. Stevo just wanted more of Jenny.

After slamming the Monaro's door shut, Stevo screeched up and down the street just to let everyone know who they were dealing with. Unfortunately he chose to do this in an area where the Neighbourhood Watch was highly motivated, thoroughly trained and heavily financed, coming under the expert guidance of retired army officer, Colonel Loader. In next to no time the negotiating team had Stevo sitting in the gutter crying his eyes out without needing to bring in the helicopter or the dog squad at all.

'Good morning, Eric.' Mrs Underwood was coming out of Jenny's room.

'Is Jenny okay?'

'Yeah, she'll get over it. She's not going back to tech though.'

'What's she gonna do, Mum?'

'I don't know. Why don't you go and see her?'

'No way. I'm not going into the dragon's lair.'

'Go on, she'd like to see you.'

'Are you kidding? Is she sick or something?'

'Eric, go and see your sister!'

'Okay, Dad. But if she kills me, it's your fault.'

Eric nervously tiptoed towards Jenny's bedroom like a mouse approaching a home for stray cats. Normally to be caught in Jenny's room would be punishable by death. But these were not normal times. His sister was hurting, and having felt the icy hand of separation three times himself these holidays, he wanted to help.

He gently prodded the door open and half expected a pride of lions to leap on him. He even considered taking a chair in with him to help fend her off. But there was not even a whimper coming from the sad creature lying hurt underneath the covers.

'Hi, Jenny.'

'What do you want, Eric? Come to gloat have

you?' Her tone was harsh but lacked its usual sting.

'No I just wanted to see if you're okay.' He was going to say something about Stevo the Rev being a complete and utter moron but, as he was new to this situation, wisely decided to keep his foot out of his mouth. If there was going to be any abusing done, Jenny should be the one to do it. 'Would you like a cup of tea?'

'No thanks.' Jenny turned towards him and Eric could see she was hugging her Sweepy Bear that she'd been given for her first birthday. 'You never likd Stevo did you?'

'He was okay.'

'Oh come on Eric! Your nose is getting bigger.'

'Well he left me at the shops that time.' Eric was referring to the time that he and Jenny caught a train in to Parramatta to do their Christmas shopping. They'd bumped into Stevo the Rev at McDonald's. He wasn't Christmas shopping but generally hanging out. He'd given Jenny a lift home but Eric had to catch a train on account of Stevo having Mr Sheened the back seat the week before.

'I guess that was pretty slack.'

'I got over it. You're not going back to tech?'

'You must be kidding, I failed grease and oil change one.'

'What are you gunna to do?'

'Dunno. I'm thinking of going back to school.'

'Yeah that'd be great. We'd be at the same school.'

'Of course it does have its drawbacks.'

'Would you repeat year eleven or would you be able to catch up?'

'I think I'd be able to catch up.'

'Yeah your three unit needlework class couldn't have moved too far ahead,' said Eric, finding another use for one of his father's priceless quotes.

'Eric?'

'What?'

'You stink.'

'So what, you caused it.'

'Come here, Eric!'

'Why?'

'I want to give you a hug.'

'Do I have to?'

'Yes you do.'

As Eric hugged his sister he had never felt so close to her in all his life, and had to work hard to fight back a tear. The honk of a car horn caused them to separate.

'Who's that?' Eric immediately knew that it wasn't Stevo. It was a simple honk, not the sound of a reggae band coming from under the bonnet.

'It's probably the puke police coming to arrest us for being so schmaltzy.' Jenny was not normally given to emotional displays amongst the family, but her reply made Eric smile.

'Oh no. It'll be Mrs Suede. She asked me if I wanted to see her off at the airport.'

'How will you get home?'

'She's paying for a taxi.' And with that Eric bolted out of Jenny's lair and quickly threw on a pair of jeans and a T-shirt.

'Eric, take a jumper with you. It gets cold at the airport.'

'It doesn't get cold at the airport, Mum. You just say it gets cold everywhere.'

'Take a jumper Eric, just for our sake,' said his father.

'Okay but not the one with sheep on it.'

'What's wrong with the one with sheep on it? It used to be your favourite.'

'Yeah, Mum, when I was five: I'm almost thirteen now. The sheep one's embarrassing.'

Mrs Underwood disappeared into Eric's bedroom and came back with a jumper that had moo cows and horses on it. Eric felt that his mother had missed the point but took the jumper anyway as Mrs Suede was going to wear the horn out any minute.

On the way to the airport Eric chatted non-stop about Mrs Suede and Iggy's new life in London and how he looked forward to visiting one day. For once Mrs Suede shared Eric's enthusiasm and talked eagerly about the novel that she'd started work on since they'd last spoken. She looked about ten years younger.

Eric had a question about Mrs Suede's car slowly formulating in his head. But when they got to the airport car park, Mrs Suede got her luggage out of the boot, threw the keys into some bushes and simply abandoned it.

'I was wondering what you were going to do with it,' said Eric.

'I'd give it to your sister but it failed rego a couple of years ago and I haven't really bothered with it since. And besides it only has first and fourth gears.'

'Is that why we were jumping around so?'

'Yeah, is your neck okay?'

'I'll put some Dencorub on it when I get home.'

The airport was weird. It was mostly people arriving, people leaving, people crying, and people consuming vast amounts of alcohol. Eric couldn't quite work out the connection, but he was fairly confident that the people crying were the ones who weren't actually going anywhere.

After kissing Mrs Suede goodbye and making her promise to make Iggy write, Eric bought himself a family block of dark chocolate, went out onto the observation deck and fell in love.

Standing out on the tarmac with its four engines purring and a big kangaroo on its tail was Eric's future. Although his parents had once taken him to see his English grandparents, he was only two years old at the time and could not remember. As far as he was concerned this was the first time he'd seen a 747 up close.

His eyes panted, his tongue watered, and while his body was obviously in a confused state his mind was functioning perfectly as he looked in awe at the machine he swore that one day he'd pilot.

Eric didn't care if people laughed at him when he put on his horse and cow jumper. And although it was freezing cold out on the observation deck, he just wanted to be left alone with his future.

He spent the next hour watching various arrivals and departures and when Mrs Suede's plane taxied out a few minutes later he gave it only a cursory wave as there was another bigtop on its final approach.

Eric arrived home quite late in the afternoon.

He'd rung home earlier and said that Mrs Suede's plane had been delayed and that he wanted to wait until it had taken off. The truth being though that Mrs Suede was probably halfway to Singapore by the time he waved to his last plane and jumped into a taxi. Eric had to show the driver Mrs Suede's thirty dollars before he would agree to take him anywhere.

After Eric had finished telling the family all about the planes and how he intended to become a pilot, he was immediately jerked out of his aviation heaven in no uncertain terms.

'Eric can you try and make your pyjamas last a bit longer? I seem to be washing a set every other day.'

'Yes, Dad.' Eric immediately slunk off to his room. He'd dreamt about Liz the night before and it had happened again.

'Roger? Did you say you were washing a pair of Eric's pyjamas every second day?'

'Well almost. Why?'

'Well maybe it's because . . .' Eric didn't hear the rest of what his mother said because he'd closed the door and was busy looking for a hole to die in.

Eric was surprised five minutes later when his

father came into his bedroom. 'You know what I was saying before about making your pyjamas last? Well, forget it. Put as many in the wash as you like. In fact I don't think you've got enough. There's some on special at Big W at the moment and I'll buy you ten new pairs if you like.'

'Okay thanks, Dad.'

'Yeah. You put a couple of pairs into the wash each day if you like. Five, six, eight pairs, it doesn't matter me or your mother.' His father had quite clearly lost it.

Eric couldn't understand what was behind his father's anxiety. He was just glad that whatever it was he appeared to be off the pyjama hook.

With the load of damp pyjamas lifted from his mind, Eric opened his curtains and jumped onto his bed. He had a wonderfully relaxed nap, his body bathed in glorious sunshine.

Chapter 9

The Underwood household was chaotic at the best of times, but reached new levels of bedlam on the first morning of the new school year.

'Have you got your paste, Eric?'

'Mum, I'm going to high school. I won't be needing any paste.'

'What about your crayons?'

'I've got them.'

'Mum, where's my Snoopy drink bottle?'

'In the freezer, Paul. You don't need it yet. C'mon, Jenny, get up! You don't want to be late on your first day back.'

'Don't I?' said the half-person-half-doona from the second bedroom.

'Roger, can you help? At least get Paul sorted out and put the kettle on!' said Mrs Underwood to her husband.

'Okay, Beth. Give me a broom and I'll sweep the floor as I'm walking around as well.'

Eventually some order was dragged from the chaos and the three Underwood children, who were all at their own educational crossroads, were despatched to their various schools.

Eric's parents had taken the day off work to get him started at high school, and Paul at kindergarten. Jenny decided not to accept the offered ride and had chosen to walk, feeling that to be seen arriving at school with the oldies would bring mega embarrassment.

'Eric, if somebody asks whether I'm your sister, deny it!'

'Okay, Thing. As long as you do the same.'

About an hour later all the new year seven students and their proud parents were sitting in the school auditorium generally beaming at each other and being waffled at by various speech makers.

'Why do these things drag on so much?' Mr Underwood was eager to get his sons sorted out and head to the golf course.

'Quiet, Roger! This person is very interesting. He's been given the key to the door of the city.'

Mr Underwood turned to Eric. 'The way the crime rate is going, maybe they should have given him the crowbar to the window instead.'

Eventually the speeches ground to a halt and the students simultaneously tried to clear out at once to avoid being kissed by their parents.

Eric gave Paul a high five, told his mother to enjoy her day off, and warned his father about the fairway bunker on the sixteenth, before he joined his new classmates in the higher halls of learning.

Chapter 10

'All right, all right, settle down!' said the teacher as his new students took their seats. This confused them slightly because they weren't making a sound.

Mr Lawrence was forty-five, fat, and a lot of fun. He wore a permanent smile around his lips and a brightly coloured bow tie around his neck.

Eric was glad that he got Mr Lawrence as one of his teachers. He had heard all about him from Iggy and Jenny.

According to them, Mr Lawrence had fought in the Vietnam War. Rumour had it that he was injured by one of those anti-personnel mine things. And if the rumour was true, he arrived back from the so-called 'policing action' minus his sexuality.

Mr Lawrence was probably the most popular

teacher in the school. Apart from being an absolute cack, he'd once stood up to three bikies who were hassling a year eleven girl down the bottom oval. Apparently he held all three of them in a headlock while the four male PE teachers went to phone the police. They were such wimps. Mr Lawrence may not have had any testicles, but he certainly had a lot of balls.

'Oh, you're not making any noise. Well, one of us was, it must have been me then. All right, that's afternoon detention for me, and if I do it again I'll have to send myself to the principal's office.'

A couple of his students laughed, while a few more looked at him as if he were mad.

Eric was one of the ones who laughed, having been brought up on his father's sense of humour, which was very similar.

'My name is Lawrence of Arcadia. No it's not. Let me just check my notes here a minute.' Mr Lawrence fumbled with some folders and bits of paper on his desk. Some of the more nervous students started to relax.

'Ahh here it is. My name, according to the available evidence, is William Lawrence, but you may call me Mister, and I apparently come from Arcadia. Ahh well, that seems to have sorted out who I am. Now what about all of you, umm? I believe I'm supposed to mark the roll. Such a tedious task. Okay, let's try it this way. Is there anybody here who shouldn't?'

The students were somewhat confused.

'Mmmnnn. This particular method does have its drawbacks.'

Mr Lawrence proceeded to mark the roll in the usual way. It was very clear that his students were enjoying their new school.

With the roll marking complete, he handed out a textbook to each of them.

'Apart from being allocated the monumentally brain-taxing task of marking the roll each day, I also double as your English teacher. Now, hands up those who speak English!'

Class 7.A4 looked around the room and slowly raised its collective hand.

'All of you already speak English? Well that's made my job a heck of a lot easier. All right then, no point wasting time. Class dismissed for the next six years!'

Mr Lawrence started to tidy up his desk as if he was getting ready to leave.

'Err, Sir?'

'Yes, what is it?'

'Aren't you meant to teach us about poems and stuff?'

'What's your name?'

'Eric Underwood, Sir.'

'Eric Underwood Sir? I don't remember marking your name off the roll. Let me check. Nope. There's nobody by the name of Sir on my roll. Are you sure you're in the right place?'

'Yes, Sir. It's just Eric Underwood, not Eric Underwood Sir, Sir.'

'I think we had better stop this conversation, Eric, before one of us gets confused. Probably me.'

'Well, our friend Mr Underwood seems to think my task is to teach you more than to speak English, and that I am charged with the responsibility of teaching you about, and I quote, "poems and stuff". Let me check.'

Eric cringed at his desk. He wanted to do well in English so he could impress Iggy in his letters. But why had he been so dumb as to say 'poems and stuff'? He could already feel the icy stare of his new classmates cutting into his back.

'Mr Underwood is quite correct. There is of course more to a language than just being able to speak it. Apart from improving your linguistic skills I hope that high school English will show you that literature can soar and swoop like an eagle and yet crash and roll like the thundering ocean.' Class 7.A4 clearly had a teacher who loved his subject. 'Billy Nelson, please open your textbook to page four and read aloud the poem that you will find there by Mr Spike Milligan entitled *On the Ning Nang Nong*. Oh, and Billy, please try not to make the person in front of you faint with your nicotine breath.'

'Sir?'

'I find, Mr Nelson, that boys who sit up the back invariably think they are tough customers. On top of that, you've got cigarette ash all over the front of your shirt. These two facts alone makes me think that you and I will have to keep an eye on each other this year.'

Billy Nelson wiped his shirt.

'There is no ash, Billy. But the fact that you wiped your shirt tells me you expected some to be there. You will find, class, that very little escapes my attention. We will have a good year together if you keep that in mind.

'Misters Nelson and Fern, if you want to poison your lungs that's your business, but why should the rest of us have to put up with sitting next to a couple of walking ashtrays? Don't ever come to our class reeking of cigarettes again! Is that understood?'

'Yes, Sir.' The godfathers of Toongabbie Public were clearly going to find high school tougher going.

'Now Billy, the poem if you would.'

'On the Ning Nang Nong where the Cows go Bong! And the Monkeys all say Boo! There's a Nong Nang Ning where the trees go Ping! And the tea pots Jibber Jabber Joo. On the . . .' and as Billy Nelson read the poem, Eric gave himself a low five under his desk. He felt that he had made a good start to high school, and firmly believed that he had impressed Mr Lawrence, while Billy Nelson and Greg Fern had got off on the wrong foot.

The next period was Maths. Since it wasn't one of his favourite subjects, Eric sat at the back of the room to avoid any unanswered questions that hung in the air towards the front.

Being at the back allowed Eric time to have a look around. He did a brief inventory of his new classmates.

Apart from Billy Nelson and Greg Fern, there were a few other students from Toongabbie Primary in the class, so he felt quite at home.

Eric noticed, as he looked around the room, that

there were a fair few sportheads and science brains in his new class. Labelling boys was dead easy. There were those who always got picked for teams first: the 'sportheads'. Then the ones who couldn't kick a soccer ball straight in a million years but could work out its circumference: the 'science brains'. And those who weren't particularly good at anything but just sort of drifted along and made up the numbers: the 'veggies'. The girls were not as easy to categorise and he crudely labelled them the 'haves' and the 'have nots'. Despite her goddess-like face, Sunflower Fox was a have not. On the other hand, Liz Campbell was definitely a have. It must have had something to do with her being an artist. Artists were heavily into that sort of thing.

Eric remembered the time that his parents had taken the family up to the Blue Mountains to see Norman Lindsay's gallery. Eric had always thought himself a bit of a deviate because he liked perving at girls. He couldn't believe it when he got to Norman Lindsay's place. The guy was obsessed. Eric had to take a couple of cold showers when he got home.

Even though Eric and Sunflower were a pretty hot item, she'd never let him have even the briefest peek under her sari. And all he'd seen of Liz was her naked ankles when he was hiding under her bed. He'd imagined that nakedness didn't stop at her ankles but carried on up to her hat. Which it probably did.

The thought about being in the same room with Liz while she was naked caused a cold shiver to run up his spine, and warm shivers to run down to other bits of his body. He decided that he'd better stop thinking about Norman Lindsay's gallery and the women in his life, otherwise he'd have to walk to the next lesson with his backpack covering his groin.

Instead he thought about his own position. It was a much safer subject.

Being the athlete that he was, Eric felt more at home in the company of sportheads. But seeing his mother made him wear grey pants rather than Levis, he was certain that the other kids in the class would align him with the science brains. He didn't care if they did. If he was going to be a pilot he would have to get involved in science and clever stuff. He was even considering investing in a compass. He wished he'd paid more attention to Ian's ravings about science and that when they were down the creek. If he had he'd be in a better position to accept his science-brain label. He didn't care anyway, it was better than being called a veggie.

With this resolved Eric sat smugly at his desk with the look of someone who was destined to top every subject, except Woodwork, and then go on to be crowned school athletic champion. He was even thinking about reciting his own poetry to all the love-sick good-looking girls in the class. Yeah. Yeah and then . . .

'Excuse me, are you with us?'

'Uhh, sorry Miss?'

'Apparently not. I said, "Are you with us?" '

'Oh, yes, Miss.'

'I agree, your body is definitely present. I was wondering if you minded very much bringing your mind back from whichever dimension it is currently in?'

'I'm sorry, Miss, I didn't understand wha . . .'

'*Pay attention!*'

'I was.'

'Well, if you were, perhaps you would like to answer the question that seems to have everybody else stumped?'

Eric could feel every single eye in the class trained on him.

'Well, I'm waiting. Do you know the answer?'

'Yes, Miss.'

'Well, then, what is it?'

Eric could not believe himself. Firstly he said he had been paying attention, when he clearly hadn't. And now he said he knew the answer, when in fact he hadn't even heard the question. He could feel the hole that he'd dug for himself getting deeper and deeper.

'*Well*?'

'Pythagoras,' said Eric.

'Very good. I didn't think anyone would know that. Yes, class, the Greek mathematician whose theorem you will study closely while you're at high school is, as Eric has said, Pythagoras.'

Eric could not believe it. He'd heard of Pythagoras, sure. According to Iggy he was this boring Greek dude who was heavily into angles. But he hadn't heard the question so he'd simply taken a guess.

Eric continued in this same vein for the rest of the day. He seemed to lead a charmed life. He knew a lot of the questions that were asked by his teachers, one of the other boys called him Einstein, and he was positive he heard one of the girls compare him to Tom Cruise.

He practically skipped home in the afternoon, and told his parents that they should start filling out university enrolment forms sooner rather than later. He couldn't have had a better first day if he had tried, and as he sat reading in bed that night you could have jump-started a car with the glow of confidence that beamed from his body. But there was something in the back of his mind that kept nagging, so much so he couldn't get too excited about his first day's performance. The next day was PE and he would have to reveal the bod.

Chapter 11

High school change rooms are designed to do one thing: bring mega-embarrassment to anyone who happens to own a body which he or she is slightly ashamed of.

Eric's primary school nickname of 'Spaghetti Legs' had so far failed to put in an appearance at Pendle Hill High. This was partly due to the fact that his legs were out of view in his grey school pants, but mostly because everyone was still finding their own feet and hadn't settled in well enough to start any verbal abuse. Eric felt sure that it was only a matter of time before someone caught a glimpse of the spindly trouser fillers that he called 'legs' and his body would come under fire again.

At primary school the students used to wear their casual gear to school on sports day, but clearly high school demanded a little more. Before he could show everyone what an athlete he was, he would first have to get changed in front of his peers. And that was death.

The tension at facing the third-period PE lesson was momentarily relieved when Billy Nelson tried to give the Bunsen burner a little turbo power during Science. Unfortunately he scorched the seat of his pants and needed attention from both the school nurse and the Advanced Needlework group before he could return to class.

Eric's heart almost pounded through his chest when the bell rang for the end of second period. He followed his classmates in a zombie-like trance as they led him towards his moment of truth in the change room from hell.

Like most things in life, if the worst is expected it never really eventuates. Thanks to a combination of raised towels and flailing arms, Eric was able to get changed in something like two seconds and was out jogging around the field with his legs well hidden in his tracksuit pants long before most of the other boys had undone their shoelaces.

'Alrrright lads,' said Mr McManus, the PE teacher with the immense limp. 'I want ye to rrrun thrrree laps arrrround the oval to warm up.' He and his limp had emigrated from Scotland about thirty years before and yet he could still pull off the sort of accent that even an Edinburgh-living, bagpipe playing, haggis eating, caber tossing, Loch Ness monster spotting Scotsman couldn't get away with.

When the boys had finished their three laps he called them in. 'Alrrright, lads, pay attention! This is a ball, and this is a foot, and what do ye get when ye put them together?'

'A goal,' offered some sporthead.

'Nay, that's not what am looking fer.'

'A sore foot,' suggested a science brain.

'Ye don't get a sore foot.'

'I do.'

'Well ye canna be kickin' it rrright.'

'Team work,' said a sporthead.

'Sometimes, but nay, not always. C'mon lads, it canna be too harrrd. What do ye get when you put a foot and a ball together?'

'A ball foot,' hypothesised a science brain.

'A ball foot ye ijit? What the devil's a ball foot? Football's the word I'm looking fer. When ye put a foot and a ball together ye get football, not a bloody ball foot.' It was clear to Eric that Mr McManus believed in starting with the basics. It was also abundantly clear that he was going to have to tolerate PE until the athletic carnival came around, where he could at least reveal his true sporting prowess. Until then he was just going to have to accept being labelled a science brain. But despite all that, he couldn't believe he had said 'ball foot'.

When the lesson was over, Eric power-sprinted back to the change rooms and changed in about eight seconds.

At lunch he sat with his new group. He hadn't any real friends his age now that Ian wasn't around, and found himself sitting with the three other boys from his class who shared the common bond of daggy grey pants.

When he was a sporthead at primary school his lunchtime conversations were mostly about girls, football, and avoiding school work. Now he was one of the science brains he found the conversation was centred on girls, football, and doing school work. Eric was confident that if he was going to be a pilot when he left school, this was the group to be in. He even thought about leading it.

'I think we should elect a leader,' said Eric.

'Of what?' Noel Stevenson was the owner of a heavy-duty pimple problem and Dolphin torch.

'Of this. The group.'

'I don't believe in leaders, but then again I don't really care,' said Stephen Brown. He held strong views on both anarchy and apathy.

Eventually Boyd Bannister was elected leader of the group. They surprisingly decided to call themselves the 'Science Brains'. They figured if people were going to call them that anyway, they might as well take the bull by the horns and beat them to it. Eric was elected vice-president to the vice-president, Noel Stevenson. They decided to act on Eric's suggestion that anybody who scored less than ninety per cent on a math's test was automatically out of the gang.

The next few weeks went smoothly, in fact Eric could not believe how great school was. He constantly impressed Mr Lawrence with his references to Chekhov and Gandhi, the Science Brains seemed to be topping every subject, and Eric's legs or lack of them had so far remained undetected in the change rooms. He had also fallen in love again with an absolute goddess in brown socks from his class called Veronica Roberts. Life could not have been better.

But over the following weeks the winds of change swept through Pendle Hill High and things began to slide.

Chapter 12

Six weeks into the first term Eric sat in class wondering where it had all gone wrong. It was his birthday, but nobody seemed to care too much, so he acted as if he didn't either. He had hoped that Veronica Roberts would come and sit next to him, give him a birthday card and a big sloppy wet kiss with a bit of tongue thrown in as well. But of course even allowing for Eric's wild dreams, which included all day pashing sessions with both Sunflower and Liz, this was taking daydreaming to the absolute max.

English was the first lesson after lunch on Fridays but he wasn't even able to run around at break time because it was raining and surprisingly cold for that time of year. He'd spent the lunch break alone in the library trying to acquire both knowledge and warmth.

He was officially out of the Science Brains thanks to scoring a meagre twenty per cent on the first math's test. He wasn't that bad at maths but had simply 'trued' where he should have 'falsed' and vice versa. Iggy had a loosely tested theory, which Eric often followed, and that was the answers to a true or false quiz usually followed a set pattern; that is, the first answer is 'T' followed by two 'F's, this in turn is followed by a 'T' then an 'F' and then three 'T's just to get you excited. The theory was that the quiz could be answered like this without the tedious need to actually look at the questions. It had served both Iggy and Eric well in the past, and it might have even worked this time. But Eric had failed to take into account that only the first ten questions were of the true or false variety; the remaining thirty required some degree of mathematical involvement. So out of the Science Brains he went, thanks to his own rule. He didn't like the way the rest of the gang said they would make a special consideration for him. He didn't like the implications of that at all. The fact that they had mentioned it seemed to indicate that he didn't belong in the gang in the first place. And while the math's test seemed to support this theory, it did nothing to calm Eric's anger towards his former friends. On top of that Veronica Roberts was going with Boyd Bannister, the leader of the Science Brains, who had apparently wooed her by doubling her home in the rain on the back of his bike while quoting from Shakespearian tragedy.

Eric realised that without any effort on his part, he had become the class dag. He could even feel his top front teeth starting to stick out, and he had to fight off an overwhelming urge to go out and buy a couple of ABBA records.

He wasn't brainy enough to get away with grey pants, and he wasn't quick witted enough to toss in any funny lines that the rest of the class would laugh at. He was caught in a kind of classroom blind spot and there was no escape.

He had no friends. The girls looked right through him. He'd smashed a mallet to bits in Woodwork and was not allowed to touch any tools other than sandpaper. On top of all that he was coming last in Maths, his 'ball foot' blunder had earned him nothing but ridicule every time he saw Mr McManus, and to make matters worse he couldn't even impress Mr Lawrence any more since he'd had a nervous breakdown and was carted off uttering something about choppers.

Nobody picked on Eric, they just ignored him, which he thought was worse. At least when he was being picked on his existence was being acknowledged. Now the whole school seemed to be part of a plot to look right through him. So he started spending his school breaks in the relative sanctuary of the library, and his time at home tucked under the safety of his doona.

Eric gazed out of the window in English and wondered what he could do to bring himself to the attention of his classmates again, particularly that babe Veronica Roberts. He had to be careful, though. The last time he'd tried to attract instant fame had brought nothing but trouble. It was during a fourth grade lesson on frogs that Eric had begun to feel himself drifting into the background. In an effort to make himself noticed again, at the end of the lesson he announced, in a loud, confident voice, that he could outdo the Bush Tucker Man, Densey Clyne or anybody else for that matter when it came to amphibians. In order to prove it, he was going to catch a record number of tadpoles from Toongabbie Creek. Unfortunately he didn't think this through clearly, the end result being one hundred very confused frogs hopping around the Underwoods' backyard a few weeks later. It had taken him forty-seven trips to the creek before they were all finally deported.

Then there was the time before that when his third grade class were staging *Pygmalion* for the school concert. A couple of Eric's classmates convinced him that he'd got the main part. He raced home and told his parents that he was going to be the star of *Pygmalion*, and that he would be playing the part of the pig. They spent the next half an hour rolling round on the carpet in fits of laughter. They were such dags. It was a while before Eric told them anything again.

Eric had to admit that the *Pygmalion* and tadpole incidents had been disasters. This time he would have to find something that didn't involve anything slimy or stupid sounding plays. And then it struck him what he would do. It had been there all along! Instant fame was his for the taking like it had been since his family had moved to Toongabbie. In the past he had been too young and scared. But now having turned thirteen, he reckoned he could handle it.

'I'm going to cross the Pipe of No Return,' said Eric out loud. A few of his classmates started to laugh.

'Excuse me?' said the relief teacher.

'Oh, ah, I'm sorry, Miss.'

'What did you say?'

'Nothing, Miss.'

'Now come on: you sit there day after day and we never hear a peep out of you and then you suddenly blurt something out. I for one would like to know what it was.'

'I said that I was going to cross the Pipe of No Return.'

'What's the pipe of no . . .'

'Don't be stupid, Underwood! A little wooss like you wouldn't have the guts.'

'You wait and see, Nelson. I'll show you who's a wooss.'

'Are you called me a wooss, Underwood? You little loser.'

'If the cap fits, moron.'

'You wait, Spaghetti Legs. You're dead.'

'When you two are quite finished the rest of us would like to get back to the lesson.'

'Not really, Miss, let them have a fight,' said Noel Stevenson.

'Eric and Billy, outside! And if I hear so much as a squeak, you'll both be keeping me company in detention this afternoon.'

Eric walked proudly out of the room. He had

forced his way back into the attention of the class. Now all he had to do was live up to his boast and they wouldn't forget him so easily again. Unfortunately Billy Nelson stole a bit of his limelight by walking out of the class squeaking like a gigantic mouse.

'Iggy Suede is not always going to be around to protect you, Spaghetti Legs, and when he's not, you're mine,' whispered Billy out in the corridor. 'And if you think what he did to me and Ferny was bad, just wait till you see what we've got lined up for you.'

'Billy, is it just an ugly rumour or are you really sleeping with Greg Fern?'

The chase went through B-block, under C-block and over A-block before they were finally collared on their third lap around the auditorium.

'That'll be thrrree days' detention for both of ye,' said Mr McManus as he dragged them back to class by their ears.

Eric was suddenly enjoying school again.

Chapter 13

Crossing Toongabbie Creek, not too far from Eric's house, is a yellow pipe. Eric could never find out what this pipe was for. But judging from the discoloured waste that billowed from some of the smokestacks of the nearby factories, he wouldn't have been too surprised to discover that it was carrying raw mercury to dump into the surf at Bondi Beach.

The Pipe of No Return, as it was called, joined the banks at the highest point of the creek. It held a special place in the lives of all the people who hung out at the creek. Whoever was brave or foolish enough to cross it usually went down in history and had folk songs written about them. What made the pipe so dangerous, apart from its height above the jagged rocks, was that it had a plastic yellow coating which made it extremely slippery.

Nobody in Eric's class or indeed the whole of year seven had crossed the pipe as far as he knew. But he realised that if he could make it across, signing his name halfway, the class would be forced to stop ignoring him.

When he was finally released from detention in the afternoon, he raced home, put on some old clothes, collected a marker pen and raced down to the creek ready to immortalise himself.

He sat down on the pipe and made deliberate coughing noises to catch the attention of Billy Nelson and Greg Fern, who were already lighting up their first smokes of the evening.

'Ahem, ahem,' said Eric.

Nothing.

'Ahem, ahem.'

Nothing.

'Ahem, ahem.'

'What are you doing up there, Underwood?' said Greg Fern. 'You creep.'

'I told you, Fern-tree, I'm going to cross it.' Eric held out the marker pen to show them he was serious.

'If you get halfway out and panic, don't call your mummy, only the fire brigade can get you down if you get stuck, you little fag,' said Billy. He looked at Greg knowingly.

So that was it. Greg Fern had tried to cross the pipe and had to be rescued by firemen.

'Hey, Fern-tree?' yelled Eric.

'What do you want, wooss? Your teddy bear?'

'*He haw, he haw, he haw, he haw,*' said Eric, doing his best to imitate a siren.

'Get nicked, Spaghetti Legs! I bet you can't do any better,' said Greg, throwing the gauntlet well and truly at Eric's feet. And with this parting remark they disappeared around a bend in the creek where there were plenty of better places to smoke.

Eric's feet dangled around the pipe but still touched the safety of the bank. He edged out a bit further and immediately scurried back to safety.

An hour had passed since he first straddled the pipe, and in that time everything seemed to have grown wider and higher. In the long run Eric felt that he'd had enough pipe gazing for one day and went home.

He went to bed that night and thought about great achievers. His mind was blank.

He thought about having a nervous breakdown but he reckoned nobody would notice. So he got up and played computer games instead.

The following afternoon Eric sat on the pipe again, his feet and hopes dangling high above the water. The sound of the creek as it babbled over the jagged rocks did nothing to soothe him. In fact it was irritating.

Every day for the next month he sat on the pipe and stared out into uncertainty. Occasionally he would be jerked out of this hypnotic state by some smart-arse comment from either Billy Nelson or Greg Fern.

'Maybe if you sit there long enough, continental drift will help out and pass the pipe right under you,' said Billy Nelson, who was obviously brighter than he let on.

Eric didn't have a clue what he was talking about.

The pipe crossing, or rather lack of it, started to affect him. His school work, his appetite, in fact everything suffered.

One miserable Saturday afternoon Eric put on the rain gear and headed off again. It was cold, damp and horrible down the creek but he was going to fight on.

He sat in his usual position and watched the rocks disappear under the brown muddy water. The rain pelted hard against his hat.

'You're never going to cross it,' yelled Billy

Nelson. 'Why don't you go home and play with dolls?' And with this both he and Greg Fern headed off. The rain had dampened their cigarettes if not their desire for them.

Charged with anger, Eric reached out as far as he could and took a firm hold of the pipe. He dragged himself out until he caught up with his hands. He wiped the rain from his eyes and reached out again and again until he found himself past the point of no return. It wasn't as far down to the water as he'd imagined it would be. The pipe was made extra slippery by the rain and with his raincoat wet he could slide along quite easily. The drop to the water seemed even less than before.

Terror gripped every muscle of his body as he realised that the reason it wasn't so far down to the water was that the water was coming up to meet him! He was caught in the middle of one of Toongabbie Creek's notorious flash floods. He wrapped his arms and legs tight around the pipe, too petrified to move. The noise of the rushing water drowned out his screams. Motorists, keen to get home before the bridge was washed out, didn't even see the creature clinging to the yellow pipe.

When the water began to lap against his feet

he just about gave up hope. The choice was simple: lie there and die, or try to make it to the other side. Eric realised if he chose the second option he would probably get swept to a watery grave anyway. So why bother? His left shoe was removed and he could feel the water round his foot. This was it. Death had begun to tickle his toes.

He summoned all his strength and courage and reached out, as before, to pull in a handful of pipe. A rat, swept down from further up the creek, humped itself for a moment over the pipe before being washed off into the current again. Eric managed to make his way slowly along the pipe until finally, with one last effort, he reached out and caught the branch of a low hanging tree, and pulled himself to safety. He glanced back and saw about a dozen rats scattered along the pipe now; ten seconds later it was completely underwater. Eric fainted.

The following Monday morning he sat in his History class and looked back on his brush with death.

He didn't care if the class knew that he'd crossed the pipe, he was just glad it was all over. He swore he would never go down to the creek again.

Surprisingly the pipe had revealed more about

him and Greg Fern than he could have guessed.

A kick on his chair yanked Eric out of his thoughts. He turned around and saw Billy Nelson and Greg Fern leering at him.

'A little wooss like you will never cross the Pipe of No Return.'

'You're wrong, Nelson, I've already done it. And there wasn't a siren to be heard, Fern-tree.'

'You have not, Spaghetti Legs,' said Greg Fern.

'I have.'

'Prove it!'

'Okay. Greg Fern loves Leanne Oakley, Greg Fern loves Leanne Oakley, Greg Fern loves Leanne Oakley,' said Eric in a sing-song voice. And while the rest of the class looked at the shocked face of Greg Fern and the surprised face of Leanne Oakley, Eric turned around and sat smugly looking ahead.

Chapter 14

The first term's break had loomed up quickly, and as Eric lounged about in bed on day one he thought back on his high school life so far.

It hadn't been a major success by any standards. His Pipe of No Return crossing, while not bringing him exactly fame had brought him some sort of toleration amongst his classmates, but it had nearly cost him his life.

Much to Eric's annoyance, his outing of Greg Fern's love for Leanne Oakley, that he'd found etched on the Pipe of No Return, backfired quite badly. It caused quite a stir amongst the class at first, however the end result was that Greg and Leanne started going together and became the hot item of 7.A4 when Eric desperately wanted that position for himself and Veronica Roberts who was getting better looking by the minute.

When he first saw her he thought she was cute. Now he reckoned she looked like Julia Roberts, Madonna, Demi Moore, Liz and Sunflower all rolled into one. She was a babe to the max. But unfortunately she was practically engaged to that science brained loser, Boyd Bannister.

Love life aside, it wasn't all bad during the first term. In the last week before the holidays, Stephen Brown resigned from his position of vice-president to the vice-president of the Science Brains and he and Eric became friends, 'united outcasts' Stephen called them.

They struck up their friendship when in a weak moment, in woodwork, Eric embarrassingly told Stephen about how he'd started wetting the bed again, and what the hell could he do to stop it.

'You're not wetting the bed, they're wet dreams,' said Stephen.

'What?' said Eric, trying to hush Stephen down a bit but still clearly interested.

'Wet dreams.'

Eric smiled, nodded and made a few 'ahh ahh' noises before finally giving up. 'What are wet dreams?'

'Are you usually dreaming about girls when they happen?'

'Yeah, Veronica Roberts usually, but sometimes Sunflower Fox, she was this girl from my class at primary, and there's my ex-neighbour, Liz Campbell and . . .'

'Underwood?' interrupted Stephen.

'Yeah?'

'I get the point. The question is do you?'

'No.'

'Man, you can become a father.'

'What?'

'You heard. If you did any of those things that you dream about with all these girls that your mind seems to have access to, and they were ovulating, there's a good chance that your parents would become grandparents.'

'But I've only just turned thirteen.'

'It doesn't matter. Do you think as your sperm is making its way towards the egg that it's going to turn around and say "don't fertilise me you nasty little tadpole, you're only from a thirteen year old?" No way. In the world of reproduction when you're old enough, you're old enough.'

'I thought it was a bit gooey for, well you know, for . . .'

'Wee? Yeah you're right, it is. Welcome to adolescence.'

Like Eric, Stephen wasn't allowed to touch any tools in woodwork because he'd broken the lathe and the two of them usually spent the lesson locked in the back room trying to sandpaper a bird house into shape. The end result was that they spent their time in the back room talking and making sandpapering noises in an effort to keep Mr Whittle, the Woodwork teacher, of their case.

'Er, Stephen?'

'Yeah?'

'You mentioned something about girls and ovals, what's that?'

'Not ovals. Ovulating.'

'Yeah what is it?'

'Don't you know anything about anything?'

'I know where Chekhov's buried, and what Gandhi did.'

'That must come in handy. What about anything useful? You're friends with that smart guy who lives near you, what's his name? Iggy Suede isn't it?'

'Yeah but he's moved to England. Don't tell anyone, though, cause if Nelson and Fern-tree find out, I'm history.'

'Didn't he talk to you about any of this?'

'No not really, mostly just books and music and philosophy.'

'That's really great, Eric. I bet you're a big hit at parties.'

'I don't get invited to any, I don't care eigher. How many thirteen year olds do you reckon have heard of Jean-Paul Sartre?'

'Not many. But can Jean-Paul teach you about girls?'

'Of course not, he's dead.'

'Okay then it looks like lesson two will have to come from Stephen-John.'

'What was lesson one?'

'Wet dreams, Underwood, pay attention! Have you noticed how some of the girls in class sometimes have to go and see the school nurse?'

'Yeah.'

'What do you think's wrong with them?'

'They're sick I suppose.'

'They're not sick, there's nothing wrong with them, although they sometimes get stomach cramps which can't be very nice.'

'What can't?'

'Their periods. What happens is their wombs get lined with blood but if their eggs aren't fertilised by the stuff that you are leaving about all over your PJ's, then once a month the blood's discharged and the cycle starts again.'

Eric couldn't help being impressed by his friend's knowledge. He obviously hadn't been reading Phantom comics.

'How come you know all this?'

'My mother's a doctor, she tells me everything.'

Eric stopped thinking about Woodwork long enough to go out to the kitchen and get himself a bowl of Coco Pops. He enjoyed his conversations with Stephen Brown and could hardly wait for school to start back. Despite the fact that Stephen's lessons were not on the year seven syllabus, Eric felt that he'd learned more from Woodwork than all of his other classes combined, and the mere sight of sandpaper in his father's shed caused him to get excited.

'Eric!' yelled Jenny across three rooms.

'What?'

'*Do you think we should get up?*'

'Why?'

'*It's two o'clock in the afternoon.*'

'So?'

'*Mum and Dad'll be home at five. We should at least wash the dishes and vacuum.*'

"I suppose. Where's Paul?'

'*He's staying with Auntie Dot for the holidays. The*

grumblies don't think we're mature enough to look after him.'

'He's staying there for two weeks?'

'No, retard, they're gonna drop him off every morning and pick him up at night.'

'Jenny?'

'What?'

'Will you stop yelling?'

The following day, as agreed, Stephen came round and they went out for a bike ride. Eric realised his friend, apart from knowing heaps, was either an extremely good bike rider or a hideously reckless one because as they zoomed off from the driveway, he broke a couple of laws of gravity and a few more governing public safety.

Stephen's family went away the next day so Eric kept himself amused for the remainder of the holidays by concentrating on his new hobby of Airfix kits. If Liz still lived next door he night have gone for a peek in her undie drawer. But he had to be content with building an F-18 model fighter instead. It seemed a poor second.

He went for a bike ride round to Veronica Roberts' house in the second week of the hols but started packin' it when he got into her street. Instead of knocking on her door and asking her out to the movies, he zoomed past her house and all the way back home and hid under his doona for a while.

Despite his poor attempt to ask Veronica Roberts out, he enjoyed his time away from school and the weather was great. In fact the sun streamed in past Eric's curtains right through the break and it only became a bit overcast on the very last day.

Chapter 15

On the first morning of the new term Eric realised it was back to the library for a while because Stephen Brown's holiday to the Gold Coast was for an extra week. He was also a bit disappointed to find out they had a new English teacher. He'd also learned from the gossip that the class fat boy, Paul Morris, had gone to a health farm, which meant that without him to bear the brunt of the abuse from the 'backrow boys', which included constant speculative remarks regarding the width of his backside, the attention might fall on himself.

'Miss Hemingway has found herself a permanent position at another school so I will be your English teacher until Mr Lawrence returns from Never-Never land. My name is Mr Cumming and I expect three things from you while I am your teacher.

One, do not speak unless you are spoken to. Two, all homework must be completed otherwise you'll find yourself on detention, is that understood?'

'What's the third thing?' asked Billy Nelson.

'Don't ask stupid questions!'

'I'm not. You said there were three things, but you only told us two.'

'Don't ask stupid questions is the third thing. Now, is there anybody else who feels like interrupting, or should I say detention?'

Eric felt that Mr Cumming was a well balanced sort of teacher. That is, he appeared to have a chip on both shoulders. His Mel Gibson looks ensured that just about half of the school, including the teaching staff, thought he was a total hunk, while the other half wanted to break heavy objects over him because he was so arrogant. He drove a BMW convertible and had an ego the size of D-block.

'Okay, I suppose I'd better get to know you,' said Mr Cumming, reluctantly reaching for the roll, and a few of the more impressionable girls had to wipe the drool from their mouths.

'Jenny Baker?'

'Here, Sir.'

'Boyd Bannister?'

'Yah.'

'Stephen Brown?'

'He won't be back till next week.'

'Who said that?'

'I did.'

'And who might I be?'

'You're the teacher.'

'I know who I am; who are you?'

'The student.'

'Your name, thicko?'

'Oh. Eric Underwood.'

'Well Mr Oh Eric Underwood, *don't interrupt!*'

Although he liked helping his teachers out during roll call, he was going to make an effort to keep his mouth closed for the rest of this one. Cumming was a dickhead.

'Greg Fern?'

'*Hhnfm Snirn.*'

'Take that sandwich out of your mouth, Fern, and see me in detention!'

Even though Eric loathed Greg Fern, he didn't think the dag deserved detention for having a chomp on a sandwich.

As the roll marking went on, Eric spent the time gazing at Veronica Roberts and out of the window.

'Is Paul Morris away?'

'Oh. He's gone to a health farm.'

'He's gone to a health farm what?'

'He's gone to a health farm to lose weight.'

'He's gone to a health farm to lose weight what?'

A confused look sprawled itself across Eric's face. He only wanted to help but his naivety landed him in trouble again. Why hadn't he kept his mouth shut?

'I'll try again,' said Mr Cumming. The veins in his neck were pulsating seriously at this point.

'He's gone to a health farm to lose weight what?'

Still nothing.

The tension of the roll marking was slightly relieved when the class cracked up after Paul Watson released one of his morning wake up calls into the air. But apart from telling James Lee to open a window, Mr Cumming chose to ignore it.

'Can anybody help this demented child?'

'I'm not.'

'You're not what?'

'What you just said.'

'What you just said what? Oh never mind, stick to the first point! He's gone to a health farm to lose weight what?'

'Off his thunder thighs,' suggested Billy Nelson.

'No.'

'From his tummy?' chirped Julie Douglas.

112

'No.'

'Off his backside?' offered John Kennedy.

'No! No! No! What's wrong with you all? He's gone to a health farm to lose weight, Sir.'

'He's gone to a health farm to lose weight, Sir?'

'Yes, that's it, but without the question mark. Okay Mr Underwood, you've wasted enough of my time already, now I'm going to waste some of yours. Stand outside the classroom, where I can see you, and put your hands on your head!'

Eric walked out of the room with his shoulders hung low. 'I was only trying to help,' he uttered feebly as he walked past Mr Cumming's desk, and the rest of the class cracked up again.

'As for the rest of you, if you think he's funny, please feel free to join him.'

With Eric despatched from the class and standing guiltily by the window, the marking continued.

'Now who was I up to?'

'Me, Sir?'

'And your name?'

'Zelco Zimmerman. I'm last.' The class cracked up again. Most of them had heard or come to the conclusion that despite his looks, Mr Cumming was a nasty piece of work and their laughter was a show of solidarity. Eric didn't realise it, but he'd become something of a martyr standing outside there with his hands on his head.

'You really are trying my patience boy.'

'It's Billy Nelson, *Sir.*'

'Nelson, I don't want to hear another peep out of you for the rest of the lesson.'

Veronica Roberts was next. Eric's face was flattened against the window.

'Peep.'

'Veronica Roberts?'

'Here, Sir.' Eric practically drooled when he heard her voice.

'Peep.'

'Neil Thorn?'

Eric could hear Billy Nelson's peeping noises from outside. He reckoned he was going to be in big trouble pretty soon. He was looking forward to it.

'Here.'

'Peep.'

'Eric Underwood?'

'*Here, Sir.*' A piece of chalk went flying across the room and hit Eric's head, which was poking in through the window.

'*Eric Underwood. Remove your head from the window! Put your hands back on top of it! And don't take them off until you are twenty-one, or I'll come out there and rearrange it.'*

'Peep.'

'Paul Watson? I know you're here. I can still smell you.'

'Peep.'

'Okay Nelson, outside!'

The last time Billy Nelson was dismissed from class he walked out squeaking. This time he was marched out physically by Mr Cumming, peeping all the way.

'Come here, Underwood!'

Eric walked over to where Mr Cumming had Billy Nelson pinned against the wall by his throat.

'Let him go!'

'What did you say to me, Underwood?'

'You're not allowed to touch us. Let him go or I'll report you!'

'Don't you dare try to stand up to me, Underwood!' He squeezed Billy's collar tighter and tighter just to show them who was in charge.

'You're hurting me,' said Billy Nelson, half-choked.

Eric thought he'd already bitten off more than he could chew by confronting his teacher, but he felt that he had no choice now other than to follow it through.

'Let him go, Mr Cumming, or I'll kick you in the balls and then report you.' Eric could not believe that he'd said it. But there it was out there.

Mr Cumming released his grip and a tear rolled down Billy's cheek.

'You two are a disruptive influence on the rest of this class. Miss Hemingway left a note saying that she also had cause to send you outside, so don't paint me as the villain!

'Nelson, you can stay out there for the remainder of the lesson, but I want you to think about what you've done. As for you, Underwood, you can come with me to the principal's office!'

After Mr Cumming had dragged Eric off by the scruff of his neck, Billy popped his head round the door. 'Cumming's taken Underwood to the principal's office, he's getting expelled.'

'Why?' said Leanne Oakley. She was the unofficial leader of the girls.

'Ahh umm, I stood up to Cumming but Underwood started crying.'

'You don't get expelled for crying.'

'Are you calling me a liar, Stevenson?'

'Er no, Billy.'

Mr Cumming dragged Eric down the D-block

116

stairs by his jumper and told him to wait outside the toilet. A couple of seconds later he emerged and dragged Eric inside. He pulled him into a cubicle and locked the door. 'Okay Underwood, you little smart-arse. You aren't so tough now, are you? I didn't spend four years at uni just so a little stick insect like you could put one over me. There's always a punk in each class who thinks that they can get the better of Geoffrey Cumming. I thought it was Nelson, but he's just a moron who'll leave this school and go straight to the dole office. It's the clever ones you've got to watch. They can turn a class against you. Well, come on, Underwood, you're not so smart now, are you? What do you have to say for yourself?'

'Billy Nelson's not that stupid. He knows about continental drift and stuff.'

'Oh shut up you pathetic little stick! Do you know I could snap you in half if I wanted? In fact, I've got a good mind to stuff your head down the toilet and flush it.'

'That's already been done to me seven times since I came to this stupid school.'

'You've got a real attitude problem, Underwood.'

'I'm not the only one.'

Eric felt a sharp pain on his left cheek. Mr

Cumming had slapped him hard with an open hand. Eric held his throbbing cheek. It was stinging quite badly and he could feel it turning red.

'Gandhi will get you,' said Eric.

'Gandhi? What are you talking about, you undernourished praying mantis?'

Mr Cumming opened the cubicle door and pushed Eric towards the wash basins. 'Wash your face!'

'You know something, Underwood? You're not always going to be in year seven. As much as the thought sickens me, you are going to grow up. And then when you are, say, eighteen I'll only be twenty-nine. We may meet up, and if we do we'll see if you want to stand up to me again. What do you think of that, Underwood? Knowing that when you leave school I'll be looking for you.'

'You won't be twice my age then. Or twice my size.'

Mr Cumming grabbed Eric by his hair and was about to throw him back into the cubicle when the door opened and a year 9 kid walked in. 'Get out!' yelled Mr Cumming at the poor guy whose bladder was just about to burst.

'Stay here until the red mark has gone from your face! I'll get someone to take your bag to the next class. I wouldn't tell anybody about this either. Nobody would believe you for a start.'

As soon as Mr Cumming had gone, Eric burst into tears. When the bell rang for the end of the period, he locked himself in the cubicle and spent the next hour tracing the still stinging handmark on his face and quietly sobbing.

Eric eventually caught up with his classmates halfway through the fourth period. It was Geography.

'I'm sorry I'm late, Miss, I wasn't feeling very well.'

'Don't lie to me, Eric,' said Mrs Livingstone. 'I heard all about you being sent out of class and taken to the principal's office. You should be ashamed of yourself. Sit yourself down and don't let me hear a word out of you!'

Eric retrieved his bag from Sean Keegan and sat at his desk dejected.

'You were right, Billy,' whispered Noel Stevenson quite loudly. 'He has been crying.'

Eric looked over at Veronica Roberts. She was giggling, but then again so was the rest of the class.

Chapter 16

The rest of the week went by in a blur. Eric kept his mouth closed at all times and didn't even look up from his desk during English. He couldn't work out why the class had rallied against him. On top of Spaghetti Legs, the boys in the back row, led by Billy Nelson, started calling him Cry Baby as well. And when it came to choosing between the good-looking, well-built Mr Cumming and a tall gangling introvert such as himself, there appeared to be only one choice and the girls, who never took much notice of Eric before, started ignoring the hell out of him.

Eric was slightly relieved when on the following Monday Stephen Brown got back from the Gold Coast and the two of them resumed their Woodwork lessons.

'How come you haven't got a tan?' Eric was relieved to have someone to talk to again.

'Because I'm not keen on skin grafts.'

'Didn't you go swimming?'

'Yeah, but I had factor fifteen sunscreen on, and I always put on my T-shirt and hat when I go out. It isn't sexy any longer to be tanned, Eric.'

'Veronica Roberts is tanned, and she's sexy.'

'Okay, forget that! What happened to you last week? Noel Stevenson was telling me all about it.'

Eric told his story from start to finish. Stephen's jaw did a fair amount of dropping.

'Wow, you stood up to Cumming? You're either very brave or very stupid! The guy's a nutcase.'

'I think I was stupid. But I'm sick of being picked on.'

'But he wasn't picking on you. He had Nelson in a headlock, didn't he?'

'Yeah.'

'So why'd you stick up for Nelson? He's always paying out on you.'

'I didn't do it for Nelson. I would have been next.'

'Anyway, your story is different from Nelson's and Cumming's.'

'What did they say?'

'When Cumming dragged you off, Nelson told the class that he'd stood up to Cumming and that you started crying. And when Cumming came back he told the class that he was going to take you to the principal's office, but you begged and cried so much that he let you off and told you to stay in the toilets till you stopped bawling.'

The sound of eleven saws grinding away in Woodwork was drowned out by Eric's teeth doing the same thing.

'No wonder the rest of the class is treating me like shit.'

'You've got to report Cumming to the principal.'

'He wouldn't believe me. And besides, Nelson would back up Cumming's story before mine.'

'Did you tell your folks?'

'No way.'

'Why not?'

'Cumming's bigger than my dad. I don't want to see him get hurt.'

'So what are you going to do?'

'Nothing.'

'Nothing? Are you kidding? That guy should not be teaching. Did you hear what happened at the seniors' dance last month?'

'No.'

'He got busted in the back of his car with two year eleven girls.'

'Who busted him?'

'Mr Davidson.'

'The sports master? Did he report him?'

'No, he joined in. But then a year twelve guy, who was going out with one of the girls, found them. Cumming threatened to punch him out if he told anybody. The guy's bad news. He's got to go.'

'Don't worry, what goes around comes around. You reap what you sow in this life,' said Eric, quoting Iggy.

'That's all very deep and meaningful, Eric, but meanwhile kids are getting slapped around and naive girls are getting felt up and probably worse. You reckon you reap what you sow? Well, isn't it time Cumming got a combine harvester dropped on him?'

'He'll get his. One day he's going to get some pretty heavy karma coming back at him.'

'Well, I bet that's got him worried,' said Stephen sarcastically. 'Look, will you stop talking like a hippy and get real?'

'What do you expect me to do? Bash him with a hockey stick?'

'No, not really.'

'I'm not going to fight fire with fire. I wonder what Gandhi would have done?' Eric drifted off into deep thought.

'Gandhi? Oh no, I can feel another Iggy Suede quote coming on.'

'Gandhi led the passive resistance movement against the invaders from Great Britain. The enemy had guns; they had roses. The roses won.'

'Hey, that sounds like a good name for a band.'

'I think I've got a plan, Stephen.'

'What are you going to do? Stick a rose bush up his backside and hit him over the head with a gun?'

'No. When's the next seniors' dance?'

'This Friday night I think.'

'Good. I'm going to need help from you, your sister and my sister. We'll also need a piece of paper and a crayon.'

And with Stephen looking spaced, Eric started work on the hang-glider he was sandpapering into shape. By the end of the lesson a plot was hatched and the room was thick with sawdust.

Chapter 17

The following Monday morning Eric and Stephen sat in class with a look of complete satisfaction on their faces.

'Good morning, class. My name is Miss Hardy and I will be your teacher until the end of term.' 7.A4 were going through English teachers like nothing else.

It was a great relief to a lot of students at Pendle Hill High School when Mr Cumming was dismissed following the second seniors' dance of the year.

He had been caught in the back of his car with another girl, only this time it wasn't Mr Davidson who discovered him but the principal, who was at the dance, not to score, but purely to supervise and hand out lime cordial.

Jenny Underwood had led him out to the car

park, where he caught Mr Cumming red-handed and red-faced.

Just before they got out of the car to face the music, Clare Brown handed Mr Cumming a note and gave him a kiss on the cheek.

'What's this? Your phone number?'

'Good effort!' said Clare Brown, Stephen's sister. 'The kiss wasn't from me and the note isn't either. They're from Eric Underwood.'

'What's that little creep doing sending me notes?'

Mr Cumming opened the note. It simply read: 'Gandhi got you.'

Mr Cumming got out of his car and tried in vain to fend off a tirade of abuse from the principal. If that wasn't bad enough he caught a glimpse of something bright out of the corner of his eye. He glanced over to where Eric and Stephen stood by their bikes. He couldn't see their faces though. All he could make out were a couple of white backsides mooning him through the darkness.

Eric and Stephen rode home, yelping all the way. Because it was Friday, Stephen was allowed to sleep over. Apart from getting English teachers kicked out of school, they spent the evening playing computer games and telling ghost stories until they drifted of to a peaceful sleep on a crystal clear night at two in the morning.

'Hey, Underwood!' whispered Billy Nelson, breaking into Eric's thoughts.

'What do you want, Nelson?'

'You're dead.'

'You two up the back: be quiet!' said Miss Hardy.

Billy hurriedly scribbled out a note and passed it over to Eric via Noel Stevenson.

Eric unfolded the note, which had a bit of Vegemite and he didn't like to think what else stuck to it: 'I found out that Iggy Swade moved. This arvo down the bottom field your on.'

Eric scrawled out a reply and passed it back. And as a look of anger was spreading across Billy's face, a smug one was making itself at home on Eric's. The note read: 'Swade is spelt Suede you moron, and it's not "your" on but "you're" on. Don't you pay attention during lessons? Or are you too busy playing with your girlfriend Fern-tree under the desk? As for being on this arvo, bring Fern-tree too, I'll take you both on.'

Eric knew that he was taking a huge risk. He couldn't fight for peanuts and had no desire to learn either. But after what Mr Cumming had done to him he knew he could take a couple of hits, which was all he reckoned they'd be able to get in before the crowd attracted the attention of a teacher. This would be better than being cornered by them in the change rooms or dragged into the toilets during a break.

The day fairly flew by and as Eric sat vigorously sandpapering in the back room during the last lesson, he started to get butterflies in his stomach.

'So Gandhi's taking on the two toughest guys in class, is he?' said Stephen sarcastically.

'They found out Iggy's gone. They are going to get me eventually. I might as well get it over with.'

'But you're going to fight them. What happened to Gandhi?'

'Gandhi will be there, you wait and see.'

'No, I won't be there. I'm going to tell Mr McManus or somebody.'

'Good, I was going to ask you to do that anyway. But let them get a few hits in first.'

'Why? You'll get hurt.'

'They're thirteen. Cumming smacked me in the mouth and that didn't hurt too much. How much damage can they do?'

The bell rang for the end of school and Billy Nelson poked his head into the back room. 'You're not going to chicken out are you, Underwood?'

'I'm not scared of a cry baby like you, Nelson. I'll see you down there.'

Eric looked a lonely figure as he made his way down to the bottom oval. An expectant crowd had already begun to yell for blood as the preliminary fight between two year eight girls got underway.

Some of Eric's classmates were dead against the fight and made a strong protest by not showing up. Idealism only went so far at Pendle Hill High.

Eric caught sight of Veronica Roberts out of the corner of his eye. He hoped she was there as a nurse.

The girls' fight came to an abrupt end when one of them had to break off to go to her ballet lesson. The crowd had not yet had its blood lust satisfied so it came over, surrounded Eric, and only parted to let Billy Nelson and Greg Fern through.

Eric stood in the centre of the circle and faced Billy Nelson, while Greg Fern lurked behind him like some sort of landlocked shark. Eric tried to think what Gandhi might have done when faced with a similar situation, but he drew nothing but blanks. He wondered who would start the mouthing off which usually preceded the bottom oval fights. He suddenly heard himself yell, 'Your type always think you can get the better of little wimps like me, Nelson.' He couldn't believe that he had said it and if Billy Nelson and Greg Fern weren't already waiting in line to punch him in the mouth, he would have gladly done it for them.

'Oh yeah,' offered Billy Nelson.

'Is that the best you can do, you half-wit: "Oh yeah"?'

'We didn't come here to talk, Underwood. We came to beat the living crap out of you.'

'Oh yeah,' offered Eric and the crowd cracked up. It was thoroughly enjoying itself.

Billy Nelson came charging towards Eric like a demented bull. He grabbed him by the jumper and hurled him backwards into the waiting arms of Greg Fern. Greg spun Eric round, slapped him across his left cheek and hurled him back towards Billy.

'Don't fight them,' whispered Eric to himself. 'Don't fight them. Gandhi wouldn't.'

Billy grabbed him, twisted him round and punched him in the face. As Eric hurtled back towards Fern-tree he realised that he barely felt Billy's punch. 'Don't fight, don't fight them unless you really have to. That's what Gandhi would do.'

Greg turned Eric around in a full circle and pushed him hard in the back and he flew towards

Billy. Again it didn't hurt when Billy punched him in the face and he tumbled back towards Greg.

Greg twisted Eric round again and let him have it. The crowd gave a loud 'Oooooooooo' as Greg's kick to Eric's balls made him slump to the ground.

'Stop it! You're hurting him,' yelled Veronica Roberts, who burst into tears and ran off.

Eric would have preferred her to stick around and get stuck into Billy and Greg and then come and give him the kiss of life. Even in agony he was the ultimate optimist.

He stumbled to his feet just in time to see a brown shoe planted in Greg Fern's gut. He turned round and saw Billy Nelson charging. Eric stuck out his arm as Billy ran past. It was like a giraffe running into a clothesline. Billy went down in a heap. Eric looked back at Greg Fern and saw the brown shoe connect with Greg's face. 'Oooooooooo.' He went down like a cordless bungy jumper and screamed, 'I give in, I give in.'

'You wimp, Fern,' yelled Billy, getting to his feet. 'We can handle them.'

Eric's partner came running towards Billy but Eric held up his hand. 'This one's mine.'

Billy's reputation as a tough guy was simply that, a reputation. Because he was so much bigger than everybody else, nobody had ever stood up to him before, so he'd never actually been in any fights.

Forgetting Gandhi and the fact that he thought fighting was for idiots, Eric exploded into a fury of arms and legs and threw about a thousand punches and kicks, and while he only managed to land a couple it was too much for Billy, who fell to the ground, yelling that he'd had enough.

Some of Eric's classmates came over and hoisted him high on their shoulders. But it was a hollow victory. He knew that they'd have been just as happy to cart Billy and Greg on a lap of honour around the oval had the victory gone the other way.

The crowd dispersed when Mr McManus came limping down to the bottom oval and yelled a lot of 'what's-going-on-here's' at people. By this time Eric and his accomplice were halfway home.

'You've got some blood on your nose, Eric.'

'And you've got some on your shoe.'

'Here, let me wipe it off before Mum and Dad see it,' said Jenny, reaching for a tissue.

'Thanks for your help. I'm glad the oldies made you take those karate lessons.'

'They were supposed to keep me out of trouble on the train, not the training field, but Stephen came and told me what was happening. I wasn't going to let my little bro get hurt. You should take some lessons yourself.'

'No thanks, you know I'm . . .'

'Yeah,' interrupted Jenny, 'yeah I know. You're a pacifist. But let me tell you this: it's a lot easier to play the role of a pacifist if you've got some force to back you up.'

Eric felt Jenny had missed the point, but he let it ride. He was just so grateful for her help. If she hadn't turned up, they would have probably started using him for footy practice, as the ball.

'That's two favours I owe you. Cumming and now this.'

'Families don't owe, Eric.'

Eric looked at his sister in a new light. He had always been too blinded by Iggy's brilliance to realise that he had a sister who was pretty together as well.

Eric hobbled the rest of the way home with Jenny's help. The mixture of pleasure and pain caused strange sensations in his mind and groin. Veronica Roberts had cried for him. And if that wasn't worth being kicked in the balls for, he didn't know what was.

Chapter 18

When Jenny and Eric arrived home they found their father mowing the lawn with a lot more vigour than usual.

'What's up with Dad?' asked Jenny when they got inside.

'We've had a bit of bad news from England. Your grandmother has had a fall and broken her hip.'

'Is she okay?' Eric was trying to find something sympathetic to say.

'Well, if you exclude broken hips, she's fine. We are having a house meeting after dinner though to let you know what we've decided to do about it.'

Eric went into his bedroom and tried in vain to search for an emotion that covered the broken bones of grandmothers 19,000 kilometres away. In the end he decided to play computer games instead. He felt a bit guilty about not having any feelings for his English grandmother, but he had only met her once and that was when his parents had taken him and Jenny back to the UK when he was two. They always said that he was too young to remember the trip, but Eric was convinced that his first memories consisted of vomiting over somebody in a floral dress whose breath smelled heavily of tea and scones.

But that had been eleven years ago. All he really knew about his grandmother was that she had a lot of trouble remaining vertical and she sent him an embarrassing hand-knitted jumper each year. The pastoral scenes in his grandmother's knitwear had given way in recent years to more volatile settings. The last jumper he received had a flock of starlings on it dive bombing a farmer while a vicious gang of blind mice annoyed his wife. Eric's father said that she was getting either creative or strange.

Despite Eric's lack of sadness over his grandmother's injuries, his father was clearly very upset. He was Whipper Snippering up a storm outside. Eric realised that he never really thought about his father being somebody's son. He never really thought much about his father at all. Oh sure, he was always cracking jokes and he was extremely accident prone. His most famous car accident was when he got the family up at five in the morning to drive to the beach in order to usher in the new year. When they got to Newport Beach there was only one other car in the whole car park, and it was about a kilometre away. Somehow Eric's father managed to hit it, and to make matters worse the owner of the car was innocently reading the papers inside. He leapt out and yelled, 'You've got the whole bloody car park, about two point five million spots, and you've got to come and run into me.'

'There's not much damage,' offered Mr Underwood.

'That's not the point. The fact is there are empty parking spots as far as the eye can see.'

'Yeah but for safety's sake I wanted to . . .'

'Look, I don't want to discuss it. I come down here every year to welcome the sun and to relieve a bit of stress. I don't need this.'

'Let me pay for the damage.'

'No, forget it. Just promise me you won't come back next year.'

'We were thinking of coming here every year.'

'I've been coming here on New Year's Day for the past twenty years and this is the worst start to a year I've ever had. Can't you go to another beach, preferably on the west coast?' He jumped into his car and drove off, dragging his bumper bar behind.

The sound of breaking glass brought Eric back to the present with shock.

'*Bollocks!* Are you okay, Eric?' Mr Underwood poked his head in through Eric's freshly smashed bedroom window.

'Yeah.'

'I must have caught a small rock with the Whipper Snipper. Be a good boy and get me the brush, the vacuum cleaner and a sheet of black plastic from the shed. I'll cover the window until I can get a glazier in.'

Eric realised that he was forced to stop thinking about one of his father's more famous accidents in order to help him clear up another one. And if ever an incident summed up a person, that was it.

At dinner Eric was a little nervous about attending the house meeting that was scheduled after dessert. The last house meeting that his father called was to let everybody know that he'd backed the car out over the cat.

Before dinner Eric had gone looking for the family's current cat to make sure she hadn't suffered a similar fate. He was relieved to find Kitty sunning herself on the pool cover, and to make sure that she was still alive and purring he threw a handful of water over her. He was delighted to see her leap to life and tear off in about eight different directions.

'As you all know by now, your grandmother is in hospital,' said Mr Underwood trying, from the head of the table, to project the image of the great patriarch but failing dismally because he had a bit of fried egg stuck to his chin. 'Your mother and I have decided to go and visit her.'

'What about us?' asked Jenny.

'You and Paul are coming with us. We've checked with your teachers, Jenny, and they said that you are doing very well. So as long as you take your textbooks you should be okay. We are only going for four weeks, but you are not to fall behind! Understood?'

'Yeah. No probs.'

'What about me?' asked Eric not unreasonably.

'Look, Eric, this is my mother we are talking about. If we can't get her to come out here to live this may be the last time we see her. Now, Jenny remembers her from our last visit and she's never seen Paul, and besides, if you came you'd want to go and see Iggy right?'

'Yeah.'

'Well he's in London. We are not going anywhere near London. We will be flying to Manchester and then taking a train to Yorkshire . . .'

'I'd still like to go,' said Eric.

'Don't whine, Eric! You haven't let me finish yet. We want you to stay with Auntie Dot and come up and feed Kitty and Basil and keep an eye on the place at the weekend. If you do a good job and get good grades at school we'll pay for you to spend the summer holidays with the Suedes in London. How does that sound?'

'Fantastic,' yelled Eric, forgetting Grandma Underwood's hip. 'Do I have to stay with Auntie Dot though? Can't I stay here?'

'You can at the weekends. We'll fill up the freezer before we go, and you can have Stephen stay over a couple of times if you like. But you are to stay with Auntie Dot during the week!'

After dinner Eric went into his bedroom to do some thinking. They were going away for four weeks. The damage he could do to the place in that time was immense. He had already begun to think about wild parties and all-night Freddy Krueger video sessions with Stephen Brown. But just when his overactive mind reached fever pitch, he checked himself. He knew that there was a far better plan out there. A plan that would catapult him to stardom in the eyes of his classmates. But what?

Despite his victory over Billy Nelson and Greg Fern, Eric was positive that he would still be a gangling, introverted misfit at school.

He had written to Iggy a few weeks earlier, and asked him how he could become more popular. Iggy replied saying that Eric should change and read more.

Eric took Iggy's letter out of his bottom drawer and read those words again, 'You should change and read more . . .', 'You should change and read more . . .' His family were going away for four weeks, 'You should change . . .', 'You should change . . .' Four weeks by himself, 'You should change . . .', 'You should change . . .'

The idea circled the house, 'You should change . . .', 'You should change . . .', made its way into his bedroom, 'You should change . . .', hovered above his bed, 'You should change . . .', 'You should change . . .'. *Wham*. It hit him.

Chapter 19

Dear Iggy,

Thanks for your letter which I got last week. I've thought about your suggestion but I reckon that thirteen year olds read Paul Jennings and Roald Dahl rather than Jean-Paul Sartre, but I'll think about it. Your other suggestion about changing myself though was great.

I'm sitting on my bed writing this letter having just found out the rest of the fam are going to Yorkshire for four weeks to visit my grandma who's not very well.

They've arranged for me to stay with my crazy auntie but I've already figured how I can get out of that and stay here by myself.

I haven't quite worked out everything yet, but

for the four weeks they're gone, I'm going to change, a metamorphosis I think you called it, didn't you?

I'm sorry this letter is so short but I'm really excited and I want to start work changing myself as soon as possible. See you at Christmas. (I'm coming over to see you at Christmas.)

Regards,
Eric

With the family booked to fly out on the Saturday, Eric busied himself for the remainder of the week making plans.

When Saturday morning rolled around Eric got everybody ready quick smart. As soon as they got to the airport he ushered them through the departure gates and brushed off their feeble complaints that there were still three hours to go before the scheduled flight time. Although Eric wanted desperately to be a pilot when he grew up, he had bigger fish to fry and watched only a couple of arrivals before leaping excitedly into a taxi and heading home.

When he got home he jumped onto his bike and rode round to his Auntie Dot's house. He explained that he would be staying at a friend's house rather than with her. Eric's father always said that they should put her into a home for the prematurely bewildered. It was not that she was losing any of her smarts, but rather because she was always so busy she simply forgot to do things like put out the cat, the garbage, and the fire when she left her electric blanket on all day. She was fairly gullible, and had a spare room full of Avon to prove it. When Eric told her that he would not be staying with her, she seemed more interested in tracking down the source of a high-pitched whistling sound that seemed to be coming from the kitchen. 'Oh, so you are staying with Stephen Brown. That's nice, dear. Come around for tea sometime. Who's doing all that whistling?'

'It's the kettle, Auntie Dorothy. I'll see you later.'

When Eric got home he raced round inside the house with Kitty and Basil, used his parents' waterbed as a trampoline, played his Cure CDs at full volume, and generally went berserk. He had to force himself to eat a family block of dark chocolate and a whole tub of Neapolitan ice-cream before he finally settled down.

When his stomach thawed out he started putting his metamorphosis together.

He took some ice cubes out of the freezer and the bottle of black hair dye, that he'd bought a few days earlier, from under his mattress. He got a pair of scissors from the kitchen drawer and his mother's typewriter from on top of her wardrobe. He then set about Jenny's Sex Pistols T-Shirt and his jeans with the scissors.

When his clothes had the look of being caught in the middle of a fight between a shark and a crocodile he took the hair dye into the bathroom, looked at himself hard in the mirror and said, 'Goodbye, Eric.'

About an hour later when he emerged from the bathroom there was not a blond hair to be seen. Despite the fact that he got most of the dye on the floor and vanity unit, he didn't do a bad job. Unfortunately, by the time he got back to his metamorphosis kit on the coffee table, the ice cubes had melted and he had to get more.

He numbed his left ear with the ice for about twenty minutes before sticking a sterilised sewing needle through it. When he had finished running round the house yelping in pain, he inserted one of Jenny's earrings into the freshly made hole. Jenny had taken most of her earrings to England, but Snoopy would do until he could go out and buy either a cheap sleeper or a stud from the chemist.

Eric gazed at himself in the bathroom mirror. His aim was to look like a cross between Edward Scissorhands and Robert Smith from the Cure, and although he looked more like Jana Wendt, he was still quite pleased with the result. 'Not bad, not bad. I'll get my hair cut short up the back on Monday morning and put on some mascara and eyebrow pencil,' said Eric to the new head in the mirror, 'and nobody at school will recognise me.'

When his hair had fully dried he went and put on his newly torn jeans and T-shirt, sat down at the typewriter, collected his thoughts and began to lie on paper.

Dear Miss Hardy,

~~My~~ Eric's English grandmother has fallen down several flights of stairs and is in the local ~~infrimi ifir~~ hospital. We are all ~~quiet~~ quite upset about it that's why there are so many mistakes in this letter.

Could you please excuse Eric from class for the next ~~for~~ four weeks as we ~~have gone~~ are going to visit her.

He won't fall behind because he's very smart and we've insisted that he take his books.

Yours ~~sinceerl sinceer~~
faithfully,

Mr & Mrs Underwood.

He was more than pleased with the letter and felt sure that Miss Hardy would believe it. He realised though that the letter introducing his cousin would have to be mistake free. If it wasn't, Miss Hardy might get suspicious.

The next stop was a name, a name that would reflect his new image. A name that said here's someone who's intelligent, thoughtful, opinionated, well read, and obviously a member of Greenpeace. The name was clearly going to need a hyphen or two. Finally, after experimenting with a name that had seven hyphens, he came up with the character of Jean-Paul Ramsbottom and hoped that Mr Sartre and Mrs Suede wouldn't mind too much him nicking their names.

Dear Sir/Madam,

My son Jean-Paul will be attending your school

for the next four weeks while we are visiting Australia. Unfortunately I am not able to make it to his enrolment as I am going to Canberra to chain myself to an embassy gate in order to get the United States to cut their greenhouse gas emissions.

We once took Jean-Paul to a numerologist and she said his letter is 'V'. Because of this he usually works better when he sits next to someone whose name begins with 'V'. I hope you have someone in your class called Vladamir or Veronica or something. I will be happy to discuss any of these issues with you when I return from jail.

Regards,
Joan Ramsbottom

Eric was happy with the start of this letter, even if he did get most of the facts from one of the local papers. He realised however that the second paragraph was taking things to about 9.8 on the Richter scale of bullshit and got rid of it with white-out. He would have to find another way of getting close to Veronica Roberts.

After finishing his letter he went and took

another look at himself in the bathroom mirror. He almost had to take a cold shower he was so excited.

A knock on the front door caused the bulge in his jeans to deflate slightly.

Eric hoped and prayed that it wasn't Auntie Dot. 'Who is it?'

'It's Veronica Roberts. Let me in, Eric, I want you badly.'

'It is not. It's you, Stephen.'

'Well, have you done it?'

'Yeah.'

'C'mon then, let me in! I want to see what you look like.'

'Okay. But close your eyes till you're inside.'

Eric opened the front door and led Stephen to the lounge room.

'Can I open my eyes yet?'

'Yeah.'

Stephen slowly opened his eyes and looked at Eric. 'Wow. I mean, *Wow*.'

'Do I look different?'

'I reckon!'

'Can you tell it's me?'

'If you look close you can see that it's your face, but even I had to look twice.'

'Nobody looks at me once usually, let alone twice, so I should be okay. Do you reckon I could get away with being somebody unrelated? Or do you still think I should be my own cousin?'

'McManus and Whittle would be stupid enough to believe it. But Miss Hardy and Miss Livingstone are pretty cluey. Play it safe. Be a cousin!'

'What about an injury? Do you think I should walk with a limp or something?'

'Why?'

'I'll say I've been bitten by a shark?'

'Don't bullshit too much. People won't buy everything. Did it hurt when you pierced your ear?'

'Yeah, it's still throbbing a bit. Are you staying over tonight?'

'You bet.'

To celebrate the arrival of Jean-Paul Ramsbottom, Eric and Stephen decided to have a party. They danced to Eric's Cure CDs, played full contact musical chairs, which consisted of placing one chair in the middle of the floor and then running and diving at it from opposite sides of the room. And just generally went crazy.

When daylight faded they played hide and seek in the dark before sending out for a large pizza and slumping down in front of the tv to watch a film. It was the best party either of them ever had.

They finally got to bed around midnight after falling asleep in front of the tv for a couple of hours. And as cool night breeze drifted in through the bedroom window, some 33,000 feet above Southeast Asia, Eric's mother bought another bottle of duty free perfume while his father tried in vain to get himself out of a toilet that was moving at about 900 kilometres an hour.

Chapter 20

Eric nervously edged towards the classroom like a whale approaching the coast of Japan. He tapped on the door gently and was quite surprised to hear a familiar booming voice tell him to come in.

He opened the door and a loud gasp sounded through the room. Eric wasn't sure whether it was because they recognised him or they were shocked at his appearance.

'If you want St Vincent de Paul's,' said the teacher referring to Eric's heavily slashed jeans, 'it's out the gate and ten kilometres on the right. You can't miss it, it's full of people buying safari suits for fancy dress parties.'

'I'm new here, Sir.' Eric hoped his accent was somewhere between London and Paris. Although he didn't realise it, his accent put him just to the west of Ireland. But neither the teacher nor his classmates were very good with accents and wouldn't have been shocked if they were told that the new student came from Paraguay and spoke in a forgotten Danish dialect.

Eric handed the teacher his note.

'They told me to come here, Sir, to take Eric Underwood's place. He's my cousin. We're looking after their house while they're away in England,' said Eric, lying through his teeth. He hadn't gone to the administration office at all. He'd brought the note straight to his English class. 'I'm a refugee,' he added when he felt the teacher was not digesting the note.

'Where from?'

'War-torn France.'

'France isn't at war, is it?'

'Oh umm, it's not a very big war, it didn't even make the local papers in Paris.' Eric reckoned he could pull off the lie because Mr Lawrence had been away for quite a while.

'Eric never told us he had a French cousin. Then again, Eric never told us much about anything unfortunately. Okay Jean . . .'

'That's Jean-Paul, Sir, with a hyphen.'

'Okay, Jean-Paul, do you think you could

possibly manage to wear the school uniform while you are with us?'

'We're not very well off,' said Eric, trying to pull Veronica Roberts' heart strings. 'My parents believe in bread before threads.'

Stephen, who handed Mr Lawrence Eric's first note, couldn't believe the lies Eric was coming out with. He sat visibly cringing at his desk.

'I think you could manage a pair of grey jeans and a white shirt. If not, borrow some of Eric's clothes,' said Mr Lawrence.

'Well, class, it's quite a day today. My first day back, Eric Underwood's off to England and now his cousin Jean-Paul has joined our humble hall of learning. Please take a seat, Jean-Paul.'

And as Eric limped to his desk, Stephen buried his head in his hands. He couldn't believe that they'd pulled it off.

Halfway through the lesson Mr Lawrence left the class to go to the staff room.

'Oi, spikehead,' said Billy Nelson. 'Are you really a Frenchy?'

'No. I was born in England, but my parents travelled all over Europe and I've lived for years in France.'

'Well, I reckon French kids stink. All you

Frenchys do all day's sit round eating garlic and perving at chicks.'

Some of the class started to laugh and Eric felt that he'd better answer before the mood swung against him.

'One more word from you, Nelson, and I'll knock your teeth so far down your throat you'll have to stick your toothbrush up your backsi . . .'

'That will be quite enough, Jean-Paul!' Mr Lawrence was back.

'How'd you know my name, Frog-legs?'

'Eric told me all about you, and how he kicked your backside.'

'Thank you, Jean-Paul,' said Mr Lawrence.

'Listen, Froggy . . .'

'Billy Nelson, keep your lips together or I'll come up there and staple them shut,' said Mr Lawrence. 'Just for a change, Billy, just this once, just to see how you fare, why don't you try being nice to people? If it doesn't work out you can always go back to being a moron.'

'Eiffel Tower-head started it, Sir.'

'I find that hard to believe, Billy.'

'Well he did.'

'Okay Billy, I'm not going to call you a liar directly. I'll let the rest of the class do that. Hands up those who think Billy started picking on Jean-Paul.'

After Eric had given Billy Nelson a sound beating the previous week, the rest of the class no longer lived in fear of him and slowly but surely their hands went up.

'Thank you, class. Now hands up those who think Jean-Paul started the exchange.'

Greg Fern's hand shot up. The only one.

'That's detention this afternoon for you Billy, and you too, Greg.'

'What did I do, Sir?'

'Well, it's either you or the rest of the class that's lying to me. I'm going with the numbers.'

Eric could not believe how well it was going. He was actually in the class as Jean-Paul and he could feel them all looking at him. He'd won them over. Now all he had to do was start showing everybody how clever and witty he was and a fan club would be formed for sure.

'. . . so you see class,' Mr Lawrence was digressing from the English lesson as usual, 'war very rarely solves anything . . .'

'But it's sometimes unavoidable,' interrupted Eric.

'Explain yourself, Jean-Paul.'

'The Nazis had to be stopped.'

'Agreed, but continue.'

'Umm ahhh, although pacifism helped remove the British from India and the peace activists are always singing "Give Peace a Chance", it sometimes takes more than a bunch of flowers and a guitar to stop a war. Sometimes you have to fight for peace,' said Eric, quoting from one of his father's deeper moments. He hoped Mr Lawrence would not continue too much longer. Apart from a bit about the Second World War, the pacifists of India, and the Gulf War, all memorised like a parrot from his father and Iggy, Eric knew hardly anything about the history of world conflict.

'I agree, Jean-Paul. Sometimes you have to cut out a cancer with a knife. But, isn't it better to stop the cancer from starting in the first place?'

'Yeah, I suppose.'

'Take the Gulf War for instance. Probably the most avoidable war in recent times. Well, it was billed as a battle of David versus Goliath . . .'

'But Goliath won,' said Eric, interrupting.

'That's because the biblical Goliath did not have laser-guided missiles. War is the law of the jungle I'm afraid, only the sticks and clubs of our ancestors have been replaced by technology. We turned

Baghdad into a place that Barney Rubble and Fred Flintstone wouldn't have set up home in, all to give the people of Kuwait their freedom. What about the people of Baghdad? What about their freedom? Is it their fault they've got a fruitcake for a leader?'

Eric was saved from having to answer when the bell went for the end of the period. And although he felt he had lost the debate, he was sure that he'd put in a pretty good showing and earned Mr Lawrence's respect.

The class was packing up. 'Good job Jean-Paul. I enjoyed our little verbal battle. Billy and Greg, as this is my first day back I'm going to let you off. But I do not want a repeat performance.'

Eric had to force himself to think about taking out the garbage in order to prevent a huge smile spreading across his face. Jean-Paul had definitely been a big hit with the class.

That afternoon as Eric—who, as Jean-Paul, had sawed right through the work bench—sat sandpapering in the backroom, he and Stephen thought back on the arrival of Jean-Paul.

'I couldn't believe it when you started limping,' said Stephen.

'I thought it might earn me some sympathy.'

'But you didn't limp into class, only to your chair. And you haven't limped since.'

'Do you think I should start limping again?'

'No! Just be consistent!'

'Did you see the way Veronica Roberts looked at me in History?'

'That's because you called Mrs Banks a liar.'

'She said Captain Cook discoverd Australia. What about the Aborigines? Don't they count? They've been here for 40,000 years.'

'Don't get so worked up. I agree with you.'

'Well, she was lying to us.'

'She's a history teacher. She gets paid to lie.'

'Yeah, but because I disagreed with her and said that the Aborigines discovered Australia, I get detention this arvo.'

'No, you got detention for calling her a liar. Whether she's right or wrong, she doesn't have to put up with that.'

'I reckon I've made a hit, though.'

'Yeah, you walked into class, told Mr Lawrence a pack of lies, limped to your desk, threatened to beat up Nelson in a half-Greek half-Mexican accent, argued with Mr Lawrence, called Mrs Banks a liar, and then you cut the Woodwork table in half. Great start, Eric.'

'It's better than being ignored.'

'What are you going to do tomorrow? Run naked through D-block and trash the library?'

'Maybe. Who knows? I've decided to let Jean-Paul do what he likes. But do you know the best thing?'

'What?'

'When I look at Veronica Roberts I don't feel like throwing up.'

'What do you mean?'

'When I really like girls, I can't talk to them.'

'Why not?'

'Because I'd vomit.'

'How come?'

'I get really nervous just looking at them.'

'Must be awful.'

'It is. Before I started going with my old girlfriend Sunflower, I used to almost puke every time I saw her. And then when we had this artist living next door, I spent more time in the toilet than in bed.'

'So why's it any different as Jean-Paul?'

'I dunno.'

'Well, if it is so different, why don't you ask Veronica Roberts out?'

'Oh no. I wouldn't have the guts.'

'Why not? You said you didn't feel like throwing

up when you looked at her.'

'Yeah, but there's still a big difference between not puking and asking her out.'

'You're weird, Underwood.'

'Maybe. But at least I admit it.'

For the remainder of the week Eric managed to keep Jean-Paul in the limelight by constantly arguing some minor points with his teachers. And although he was forced to wear the school uniform, he usually offset it with a pair of Jenny's black leg warmers or some equally controversial leather gloves.

Eric was glad that it didn't rain once during this time. He didn't want his black mascara to be washed off. And although the weather had been great and his change from Eric to Jean-Paul had gone very smoothly, as he relaxed in bed on the first Friday night of Jean-Paul's life he could hear the thunder clouds gathering on the horizon and felt sure that they were in for a downpour.

Chapter 21

Towards the end of the following week, Eric began to notice a slight shift in attitude towards Jean-Paul. His interruptions in class no longer met with glowing approval. Instead, everyone seemed fed up with his smart-arse comments. He didn't really care. He'd made a big hit in the playground and had become popular with the year twelve lot.

He'd got through another week as Jean-Paul but there was no doubt that people were getting used to him. He was thinking that he might have to consider a bungy jump from the bell tower in order to attract everyone's attention again.

'What are you thinking about?' asked Stephen, wrapping a new piece of sandpaper round his cork block.

'Bungy jumping.'

'What?'

'Don't worry about it.'

'Do you still want me to stay over tomorrow night?'

'Oh no, you can't.'

'Why not? I thought we were going to get a couple of videos and a pizza. Or better still a couple of pizzas and a video.'

'This girl from year twelve's having a party and I've been invited. Want to come?'

'What, listen to a bunch of morons get drunk and try to show each other how clever and funny they are? No thanks, I'd rather clean the lint out of my belly button. Anyway, I thought we were going to get *Alien* and make mega amounts of popcorn.'

'I want to go to the party.'

'Who as? Eric or Jean-Paul?'

'Jean-Paul, of course. They wouldn't have invited Eric.'

'Yeah, but Eric's a nice guy, and Jean-Paul's a dickhead, you said so yourself. Why would you want to hang around with people who invite dickheads to their party?'

'Jean-Paul may be a dickhead, but he's a popular dickhead and people like the way he looks.'

'Looks aren't everything.'

'Bull.'

'No it isn't.'

'If looks are so unimportant why do people spend so much money on perfume and aerobics and stuff? It's all bullshit. Everyone wants to look good.'

'So we're not getting any videos?'

'No. Next week maybe. If there aren't any parties on.'

'Eric Underwood was my best friend, but you got rid of him. Give me a call when he gets back.' Stephen turned his back and sandpapered up a storm.

Eric slammed down the bit of wood he was sandpapering and attempted to stomp out of class. Unfortunately his grand exit was cut off by Mr Whittle.

At about eight o'clock on the night of the party, Eric picked up the phone and dialled.

'Hello?'

'Hello Mrs Brown, is Stephen there?'

'Just a moment, Eric.'

A few moments later Stephen came to the phone. 'Hello?'

'Hi Stephen, it's Eric.'

'What do you want? I thought you were going

to your precious party.'

'I've been. You were right. They stuck me in a corner with some orange juice and then they all tried to see who had the biggest ego. I guess the novelty of Jean-Paul has worn off already.'

'Thought it might. Even Mr Lawrence is getting tired of you butting in all the time. And he knows you're getting all your facts from your father's *Time* magazines. He reads them too. I've seen him.'

'Yeah, yeah, yeah. I didn't come straight home after I left the party.'

'Where'd you go?'

'I walked past Veronica Roberts' house.'

'Why?'

'I just wanted to see if Jean-Paul had the guts to go and talk to her.'

'And did he?'

'No. He was sick in the gutter.'

Stephen was trying hard not to crack up. 'Then what?'

'He walked to the video shop and hired *Alien I, II* and *III*.'

'Eric.'

'What?'

'Put the popcorn on! I'm on my way.'

Chapter 22

The next morning Eric was woken at six by the sound of the rain pelting hard against the window. An icy wind leaked into his bedroom. The house had been permanently cold since the family left. Mr Underwood was the only one qualified to work the reverse-cycle air-conditioner.

Eric shivered as he got out of bed to retrieve the two spare doonas from the linen closet. He threw one over Stephen, who was still asleep like a hibernating bear on medication; the other he tossed over his own bed. He turned the electric blanket to level three and went back to sleep.

Stephen stirred briefly round nine and asked what was for breakfast. He went back to sleep when Eric offered to make him a snot sandwich. Breakfast was not Eric's favourite meal. He preferred to sleep instead.

When Stephen left at midday, Eric sat in front of the tv and thought about the future. He didn't know whether to kill Jean-Paul off and have an extra two-week holiday, or hang in there.

In the end he went and got the scissors and his father's razor and decided not only to let Jean-Paul live, but to update him as well.

The next morning as Eric walked into the school grounds, loud gasps could be heard from students and teachers alike. He could feel every eye in the school trained on him. He'd got them interested again.

'Don't bother te put ye bag down, laddy. Ye can come strrraight to the principal's office with me!' Mr McManus had sneaked up from behind and caught him by surprise.

After waiting in the foyer for about fifteen minutes, Eric was eventually led in to see the principal.

'Take a seat,' said Mr Power. 'I've seen you around. Name's John isn't it?'

'Jean-Paul, Sir, with a hyphen.'

'Well, Jean-Paul, I can't allow you to come to school looking like that.'

'Why not, Sir?'

'It's disruptive for a start.'

'Why?'

'At this school we have a code of conduct and a code of dress. By coming to school looking like that you are undermining my authority. I have the reputation of the school to think of. I have no alternative but to suspend you until your hair grows back.'

'I didn't mean to challenge you, Sir. I only wanted to . . . I don't know what I wanted.'

'I've just spoken to Mr Lawrence. He told me that your parents lead a different sort of lifestyle from the rest of us, so I don't think it would do any good to involve them in this. But I want you to go home and look at yourself in the mirror. Somewhere underneath that shield you've built around yourself there is an intelligent young man trying to get out. So let him out, Jean-Paul!'

Eric dragged himself back home. It had all gone wrong. He was sure that the playground would be buzzing with the news of his suspension, but it was no good to him. His hair wouldn't grow back for at least two weeks, so he wouldn't even be able to enjoy his position of martyr.

Eric crawled into bed. He was sick of Jean-Paul

and couldn't wait for Eric to come back. And with the wind and rain howling, he drifted off to an uneasy sleep.

A knock on the door woke him in the afternoon. He answered it with his doona still wrapped around him.

'Stephen, what are you doing here? It's only two thirty.'

'We're on strike. The know-alls from year twelve got together and called us all out.'

'Why?'

'Because of you. I can't believe you did it. Coming to school with your hair like that. What did you expect Power to do?'

'I don't know.'

'The school's in total chaos all because you wanted everyone to pay attention to you. Was it worth that much?'

'No. I don't want anything to do with it any more.'

'Too late. There's a meeting tonight at six o'clock. Why don't you go round and tell them to call off the strike!'

'Okay, I will.'

Just before six, Eric followed Stephen's map and rode round to Matthew O'Neil's place. He was the school captain. Eric parked his bike out the front, with all the others, and knocked on the door.

'Around the back!' said the lady who answered the door. She had a wooden spoon in one hand. Eric was sure that he could hear a metronome ticking away in the background. 'And keep it quiet! I'm trying to cook tea and give a piano lesson.'

Eric followed the path around to the back and was greeted by a sea of faces.

'Oh, it's you,' said Matthew O'Neil. 'What do you want?'

'I don't want you to go on strike over me.'

'This is not about you. It's about our rights as students.'

'But I just want to forget about it and go back to school.'

'They've said you can go back to school when you hair grows back or you can go back to school immediately if you wear a cap. But it's too late for that.'

'No, it's not. I'll wear a cap.'

'I've said this isn't about you. Just stay home!'

'Are you saying I can't go back?'

'Yeah. How can we fight for your rights to go to school if you're already there?'

'It's just like it is with the Aborigines.'

'What have they got to do with it?'

'Everyone tells them what's best for them. Nobody ever asks them what they want.'

'The Aborigines weren't doing anything with the land. It was there to be nicked. Anyway, this has got nothing to do with them, or you, it's about us. So piss off home and don't come to school until you hear from me.'

For the second time that day Eric dragged himself back home. He was going to kill off Jean-Paul there and then. But on second thoughts, why should he let a Nazi in a brown jumper boss him round? He was determined to go to school the next day even if it meant having the teaching staff all to himself.

The following day Eric sat in his English class and was delighted to see that it was a full house. Just about everyone thought that Matthew O'Neil was a dickhead before Eric's haircut. Now they were certain.

Eric had to keep the peak of the baseball cap very low now. He didn't want the secret of the Jean-Paul/Eric exchange discovered at this late stage.

When the class was dismissed at the end of the lesson, Mr Lawrence asked Eric to stay behind.

When the last of the students had filed out, Mr Lawrence told Eric to take a seat.

'When's Eric coming back, Jean-Paul?'

'I'm sorry, Sir?'

'When are you bringing Eric back?'

'You know?'

'I've known from the start.'

'Did Stephen tell you?'

'No.'

'Then how'd you know?'

'Oh c'mon, Eric. War-torn France? Occasional limps? An accent that wavers between Latvian and Bolivian?'

'If you knew, why didn't you stop me?'

'Because I wanted you to find out for yourself.'

'Find out what?'

'Who you like best. Eric or Jean-Paul.'

'Eric I suppose.'

'Before you can get others to like you, you've got to like yourself first. Eric isn't such a bad guy after all, is he?'

'Yeah, I realise that now. But I was sick of being ignored and I'm fed up with being thirteen.'

'Don't try to grow up too fast. Being an adult is overrated. These are some of the best years of your life.'

'They don't feel like it.'

'They definitely are. But you only realise it when you get to my age. Now's the time to enjoy yourself while you've still got the world at your feet. You are a very talented bloke, Eric.'

'What do you mean?'

'You created a fictional character and brought him to life. Everybody, including the principal, believed that Jean-Paul was the real thing. Channel that talent, Eric!'

'To what?'

'That's for you to figure out.'

'But what'll I do now? Should I come to school or what?'

'Are your parents really in England?'

'Yeah, that was the truth.'

'Okay, I'll arrange with your other teachers for Stephen to take work home to you. When your parents get back we will be starting holidays for two weeks, that's plenty of time for your hair to grow back.'

'Thanks, Mr Lawrence.'

'Don't take everything so seriously, Eric. Even an old fart like me enjoys life.'

'But you're not even married.' As soon as he'd said it he wanted to die. He'd forgotten about Mr

Lawrence's war wounds.

'What's not being married got to do with not enjoying yourself? I come from a long proud line of bachelors, Eric.'

Eric didn't understand the joke. He was too busy trying to work out how he could get out of the conversation without further embarrassment. 'Sorry, Sir. I forgot about your, well, you know?' He pointed to his teacher's groin to support his argument. He couldn't believe that he did it. End now, world! Please.

'Forget about what? Don't tell me that rumour is still going around?'

'Rumour?'

'The only thing I lost during the Vietnam War, Eric, was a bit of sanity, and a lot of sleep.'

'You mean you didn't get your whatsies blown off?'

'No, I did not. I got shot in the backside.'

'Did the enemy sneak up from behind?'

'No. I was trying to tear-arse away from him. A dead hero isn't much use to anybody, least of all himself. I volunteered to fight for my country, not to crash tackle machine-gun nests.'

For some reason Eric found great relief in discovering that Mr Lawrence still had all his bits.

The world needed a few more William Lawrences, and it was still capable of producing them.

For the first time in weeks Eric practically skipped home from school.

When he got home he grabbed the scissors from the kitchen drawer, went into the bathroom and took out his earring. He looked at his hair in the mirror. His blond roots were starting to come through. He hacked what was left of Jean-Paul's hair down to meet them.

Chapter 23

On the drive back from the airport Eric was delighted to hear that his grandmother was well again even if she did have to walk with the aid of a walking frame. He was also pleased to learn that his father's broken leg, the result of a tangle with the walking frame, was on the mend too. On the other hand his parents were miffed to learn that he'd been staying at home rather than with Auntie Dot. Their anger subsided a bit when they got home and saw that he hadn't completely trashed the place.

'You've been doing a bit of growing up while we've been away?'

'Yes, Mum. Quite a lot actually.'

'Good for you. You'll also have a bit more growing up to do at Christmas.'

'What do you mean?'

'When you go over to see Iggy, you'll be bringing your grandmother back with you. She's coming out to get some warmth in her old bones. Do you think you can escort her back safely?'

'Yes. No probs!'

For the two-week holiday break Eric's hair grew back under his baseball cap well out of his parents' view and his pierced ear closed up.

Being the home boy that he was he knew he could get away with wearing his baseball cap twenty-four hours a day, especially since Stephen wore his every time he came round too.

He spent the holidays reading and hanging out with Stephen, more than happy with his low profile.

Eric's return to school was not met with any great fanfare, after the excitement created by Jean-Paul. But he was glad to be back anyway.

At lunchtime on the first day, he sat with Stephen in the playground and gazed yearningly at Veronica Roberts.

Surprisingly she caught his eye and waved at him, spaghetti legs and all. He knew that she was no longer going with Boyd Bannister, but it never occurred to him that she could be interested in him. On the other hand she'd cried when Nelson and Fern-tree had used his body for a trampoline. So maybe there was hope.

Eric waved back. And even though he was back to being just plain old Eric, he didn't feel like being sick at all.

John Larkin was born in England but grew up in the western suburbs of Sydney. He has worked as a supermarket trolley boy, storeperson, shelf stacker, professional soccer player and computer analyst. He spent his younger days kicking a football and hanging round bookshops.

Australian Book Vouchers make great presents for any occasion—or for no particular occasion at all! You choose how much—$5, $10, $20, $25, or $50— and whoever you give it to chooses the book. Simple! You can get Australian Book Vouchers wherever you buy good books.